Danny and Life on Bluff Point
Revised Edition

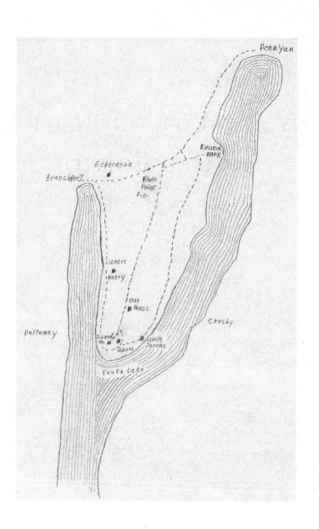

DANNY AND LIFE ON BLUFF POINT REVISED EDITION

Cougar Threat: Book One in the Danny and Life on Bluff Point Series

Mary Ellen Lee

Author of the Danny and Life on Bluff Point series of children's historical novels.

iUniverse, Inc.

New York Bloomington Shanghai

Danny and Life on Bluff Point Revised Edition

Cougar Threat: Book One in the Danny and Life on Bluff Point Series

iUniverse books may be ordered through booksellers or by contacting:

iUniverse
1663 Liberty Drive
Bloomington, IN 47403
www.iuniverse.com
1-800-Authors (1-800-288-4677)

Because of the dynamic nature of the Internet, any Web addresses or links contained in this book may have changed since publication and may no longer be valid.

This is a work of fiction. All of the characters, names, incidents, organizations, and dialogue in this novel are either the products of the author's imagination or are used fictitiously.

ISBN: 978-0-595-46407-4 (pbk)
ISBN: 978-0-595-70260-2 (cloth)
ISBN: 978-0-595-90701-4 (ebk)

Printed in the United States of America

To my loving parents, I think of them often.

Contents

ACKNOWLEDGMENTS

My thanks to Betsy Carpenter, Children's Librarian at the Penn Yan Public Library and Idelle Dillon, Director of the Oliver House Museum, for their help, support, and encouragement.

C H A P T E R 1

▼

INTRODUCTIONS

"Danny, eat your breakfast," Ma says again, this time more sternly.

It is wonderful not to have to go to school today and tomorrow. I don't want to think about my troubles there for my day at school is becoming difficult. Billy Marshall, who lives over the side of the bluff and close to the lake, keeps picking on me. His being mean to me isn't the worst part. I don't have any idea why he does it. I just don't understand what I have ever done to Billy that makes him dislike me so.

Not knowing what he is going to do to me next makes me jittery and I'm not paying attention to my class work as much as I should. I'm tired of thinking about Billy. It is getting me nowhere anyway. I do know I will have to do something about him, and soon.

When he saw me at the water pail during recess yesterday, he came by my desk and poured water on my shirt from the dipper. Thursday Billy tripped me and I fell to my knees. He helped me up but then he laughed and made fun of my size. Everyone makes fun of my size.

Billy really makes me angry and I want to do something about him but I don't know what. He wants me to fight him, I guess, but my parents taught me that people don't fight just because someone is picking on them. Besides, he is much bigger and older than I am.

Ma continues, "If you want to go with your Pa to get wood you have to eat a good breakfast."

We are all sitting around the dining table. We call our noon meal dinner and our evening meal supper. It is a big table, big enough for twelve people to sit to at one time. Now there are only six of us, Pa, Ma, my older sister Ruthie who is thirteen, I, and my younger sisters Mary who is eight, and Carolyn five. Our family name is Lee. I'm ten.

I'm very small for my age and when we are in a line by height, I'm between Mary and Carolyn. The girls love to remind me of this and just now, I discovered someone had placed the Sears Roebuck catalog on my chair! As if, I needed a boost. I dump it on the floor and try to ignore their smirks.

"What is the matter, Danny? Don't you want to be able to reach the table?" Mary giggles.

Our gray tiger house cat, Clara, is sitting in the corner of the dining room looking prim, proper, and pleased with herself. Her eyes are half closed and her front feet are braced on the floor in front of her. She is purring so loudly I can hear her from across the room. She had brought Ma another mouse this morning, which she caught in the basement. After showing it off, and meowing proudly, Clara ate the mouse, leaving behind the gall bladder and a bit of gut. She is a good hunter and that is why she lives in the house.

"Danny," Ruthie yells, "Pa is talking to you. Stop daydreaming and get back to reality, will you?"

Pa adds quickly, "You must eat now; there will be no coming back to the house until we have a good load of logs, so eat."

"Yes, sir," I say, and pour maple syrup on my buttermilk pancakes. We always have pancakes for breakfast on Saturday.

Ma smiles as I shovel the sweet maplie forkfulls into my mouth. My, but they are good! I wash the stack down with a big glass of milk.

Ma has her usual starched white apron on over her dress and her long dark brown hair is done-up in a bun at the back of her neck. Her hazel eyes sparkle as she says, "Take an apple with you for later."

I stuff one into the pocket of my heavy winter coat. There usually are apples in a big bowl in the center of the dining table. We have an apple orchard and commonly have a big supply for the winter. We keep bushel baskets of apples in the root cellar, which is off the basement of the house.

Our winter vegetables are also in the root cellar. We grow many foods in our garden, some of them Ma preserves for winter use.

Pa is ready to go and so am I. He is a tall, heavyset man with what seems to me to be the strength of two. His hair is dark and he has dramatic blue eyes.

My pants are also made of wool and are so heavy they make walking difficult because the thick fabric bunches up between my legs. I struggle into my second wool shirt and my coat. Once into my coat I can't raise my arms above my shoulders.

My hat is just like Pa's, red wool with earflaps. He doesn't have the flaps over his ears. He always tries to get out of the house in the winter without them.

However, as usual, Ma catches him and says, "Charles, you are not going out without tying your ear flaps." This while she is fixing mine in place. "You should set a good example for the children." We children enjoy hearing our Pa told what to do by our Ma.

"Yes, Ellen, you are right." He fixes his earflaps into their proper place as he winks at me. In his big hands, he has cowhide leather gloves. I have on two pairs of knit mittens. Ma always knits new mittens for each of us children for Christmas.

Two pair of wool stockings; horsehair-felt liners, which we call felts, and big rubber boots, cover our feet. The horsehair boot liners are new each year made from hair cut from our horse's tails and manes.

My boots are too big as they are new. The idea is that I will grow into them. I hope that will be soon as they are difficult to walk in being heavy and clumsy. I have some rags stuffed into the toes to make them fit better but this does not help much.

It is a bright sunny day but very cold. There is little wind, which is a good thing as the big thermometer that hangs on the outside wall of the woodshed reads ten degrees.

The door to the woodshed opens and into the kitchen walks Doc and my Uncle Ed.

"We have the team ready," Doc says.

Doc is our long-time hired hand and Uncle Ed is Pa's youngest brother.

Pa has recently given me permission to be around the men when they are doing heavy work. Farm work can be very dangerous. Much heavy work must be done by hand and the draft horses are huge.

Pa reminds me often, "Danny, you must remember the horses might step on you or bump into you if they do not know where you are. You could be kicked if you startle them. Never come up behind them and always speak to them to let them know you are nearby," he explains.

Pa has two teams of draft horses. They are a brown-red color called chestnut with lighter mane and tail. Their faces are white and so are their lower legs and feet. They are Belgians, which have great strength, endurance, and ability to pull heavy loads. I love to be around them but they make me feel so very small. The two teams are always paired together. Kit and Bess are together. Big Jim and Big Dan make up the other team.

The men treat the draft horses with great respect and care. In fact, we all treat the farm animals as if they are our friends and companions—

which in a way they are. The Golden Rule of do unto others as you would have them do unto you applies to farm animals as well as people.

"All right, let's go to work," Pa says in his deep voice.

We are going to the woodlot to bring logs to our sawmill. There they will be cut into firewood and then stored in the woodshed.

Woodstoves heat our house. There is a stove in each downstairs room except the dining room. The kitchen has a cookstove, the family parlor, and front or guest parlors each have a potbellied stove. Heat moves to the upstairs rooms by stovepipes coming up from below and by registers in the floor that allow some warmth to rise. Ma cooks with wood also.

Out through the woodshed we go, Pa, Doc, Uncle Ed, and me. There, waiting for us because this is his usual way is Buster, our collie dog who is about two years old. He is black and white with long fur. His tail is big and bushy and he wags it a lot.

Buster lives in the woodshed. He can come and go when he wishes through a hole in the end wall. A flap of heavy canvas covers the hole. I fixed a bed for him using an old quilt in a wooden box.

His job is to make sure things about the house and barns are as they should be and that there are no intruders. Buster lets us know if someone or something has come into the yard by barking a few times and running around in circles.

Buster jumps up into the air and sort of flips over, as he is happy we are outside. I give him a pat on the head and a big hug, he wags his tail so hard, and fast his whole body shakes. The men all speak to him and sometimes play with him too because they enjoy his company as much as I do.

"Hi, Buster, we are going to the woodlot, want to come with us?" I ask. Buster answers by more wiggles. Pa mostly has the dog stay at home when the men are away from the house. He is, after all, a watchdog.

Thoughts of Billy Marshall pop into my head. What can I do about him? How do I stop him from playing mean tricks on me? I'll think of some way to get back at him. I have to because this problem is making me angry. I forget about Billy for now by playing with my pal Buster.

CHAPTER 2

▼

THE WOODLOT

There has not been much new snow lately so the path to the horse barn is easy to walk on; our comings and goings have packed the snow well.

Looking ahead, it takes a few moments for me to see the two draft horses looking out at us from the barn door. I wonder which team we will be using but I don't ask a question that I can answer for myself in a few seconds. They are Kit and Bess. I recognize them because they are smaller than the male team and somewhat lighter in color. Then I remember Jim and Dan worked on Friday and would need today to rest. I'm glad we are using Kit and Bess; I don't feel quite so small when I'm near them as I do when I'm around Jim and Dan.

Kit is nodding her head and shaking her mane. She acts impatient to be getting on with her work. Bess is quiet and just pricks up her ears when she sees us. The horses look even bigger in the winter because they have their heavy fur coats. Uncle Ed easily slides the heavy barn door closed. I can hardly move it.

"Uncle, why can't I open and close this door as you do?" I ask.

"Because you are too small and don't have enough muscle. You will grow and become strong, don't worry."

"I wish I would hurry."

Uncle comes over to me and gives me a nice hug, "It will come."

The horses have on their heavy harness and are ready to get to work too. Doc and Uncle Ed lead them out of the barn and into the bright sunshine. Pa takes the reins and gently makes a clucking sound and Kit and Bess move ahead as one.

To the equipment shed we go. This building has two big rolling double doors at either end. We keep our farm equipment here to protect it from the weather. The large family cutter, the light cutter, the logging bobsled, and the small bobsled are at one end.

Doc carefully backs the team to the tongue of the logging bobsled. Both the tongue of the sled and its singletree attached to the harness. The doubletrees attach to the traces behind the horses.

"Buster, here Buster," Pa calls. Buster comes running to him and sits expectantly at his feet. "You stay home with Ma and the girls. I want you to be here to do your job and be a watchdog. Stay here, Buster."

The dog is none too happy to remain home but he seems to know this is his job. He slowly walks away and sits by the woodshed door. He looks sad and I know he wants to come to the woodlot too. Buster is not wagging his tail now.

Kit stamps her right front foot and snorts as if to say, "What is the hold up, I want to get going."

"All right, Kit, don't be so impatient," Uncle Ed laughs.

Finally, we are ready to go. Pa lifts me up onto Bess' broad back making it look like I weigh nothing. He, for what seems to be the hundredth time, reminds me, "Danny, hold on right here on Bess' collar. Remember to keep looking ahead so you will know if Bess is going to walk under a low tree limb. Pay attention and don't be daydreaming a million miles away."

I nod my head in agreement.

Doc and Uncle Ed sit on the edge of the sled with their legs hanging off while Pa stands behind the team with the reins in his hands.

Bess is just too big to grip with my legs, as I must do when riding one of our light duty horses. It is more like sitting on a chair, a big rocking chair. I hear Pa make his clucking sound and I hang on firmly.

"Giddyap Kit, Giddyap Bess," he calls. We are on our way to the wood-lot. The horses move out at their slow walking pace.

Other times of the year, our path would be along one of our farm lanes. As everything is covered with snow and there are no crops growing we use the most direct route, which is straight across last year's bean field and then across the old corn field. We join the lane there and continue to the woods.

I'm feeling very pleased with myself because I'm able to keep my seat on Bess' back without difficulty. Pa must feel I'm doing all right because he has not hollered at me to hold on. My place is nice and warm. I enjoy the odor of the horses mixed with the cold winter air.

I wonder what Pa will give me to do. Perhaps he feels I'm big enough and responsible enough to contribute to today's efforts. While I'm in school, I don't have much time to help and I want to do my part when I can. I can do plenty of things even if I am short and skinny. I just need a chance to show my skills.

Pa directs the horses to the spot along the edge of the woods where he wants to work. "Whoa girls, whoa." Kit again snorts and shakes her huge head.

These woods have many trees that are good for firewood, oak, locust, and hard maple mostly. This wood burns slowly and with greater heat than soft wood like pine or willow. Pa also uses the locust for fence and vineyard posts because it does not rot as quickly as other wood.

Pa directs the team to stop the bobsled next to big stacks of logs that the men cut early last winter. These are seasoned logs meant for firewood. The sap has dried out so it will burn with good heat. We are going to take a load to the mill house to be cut into wood stove size lengths and then split and stacked in the woodshed, ready for use.

Gathering firewood is a common event in cold weather. The men can do little on the farm except taking care of the livestock and repairing and maintaining equipment.

The men are ready to go to work and Pa helps me slide down from Bess' back.

"Danny, you unhitch the team and lead them over to that old oak tree and tie them there," Pa says.

My scrawny body suddenly feels a little stronger and I even feel a little taller.

"Yes, Pa," I reply. I try to stand as tall as I can. Here I am, responsible for about three and a half tons of horse.

I walk to the front of the team. I reach up to get the lead rope for Bess and to my disgust realize I cannot reach it. Pa's big hand unties the line and lets the end drop. Grabbing it, I follow him to Kit's side while he releases her lead line. I let the two lines drop to the snow in front of the horses and unhitch the singletree from the bobsled tongue by removing the clevis pin. Then I move to the back of the team and unhitch the doubletrees from the traces, all the while speaking softly.

The horses are following my movements with their ears. Back at their heads, I pick up the two leads and start toward the oak tree. It is a struggle for me to walk through the deep snow with my big boots and so many clothes. I very carefully tie each horse to the trunk using several half hitches. Then I step back a few paces and look up into Bess' dark eyes. She is looking directly at me. I whisper, "Oh, Bess, you are such a wonderful friend! I love you and am glad to be with you today." By this time, Uncle Ed comes along to put their blankets on.

Oh, boy, I say to myself. I hope he didn't hear what I said to Bess. "Don't you think Bess is a grand horse, Uncle Ed?"

"Yes, I do. Kit is a good horse too. But she is less patient than Bess."

"Do you think Pa will ever get me a pony of my own?"

"Suppose he will sometime, Danny."

"When do you think?"

"Donno, when he decides you are ready for the responsibility. I have to get to work; your Pa and Doc are waiting for me."

Then I remember the apple. "Would you like some apple?" I ask Bess and Kit. I get it from my coat pocket and my jackknife from my pants pocket. I never go anywhere without my jackknife.

Removing my mittens, I quickly cut the apple in two, one-half for Kit, and one-half for Bess. Munch, munch, munch. I love the soft feel of their lips and noses as they take the apple from my hand. I hope the treat will please them; I so much want them to be my friends.

I walk back to the area where the men are working and ask, "Is there anything else I can do?"

I make sure I will not be in the way while the men struggle to move the heavy logs to the sled. Pa will not ask me to do this work, as I'm not nearly strong enough.

Pa says, "You can take a walk in the woods and see if you can find fresh deer tracks and decide about how many there are in the herd. If you find them decide what their condition is." Continuing, he says, "Don't go too far, Danny."

Ah good, finding the deer is something useful and fun to do. I know he wants to know the condition of the deer herd because he needs to shoot one of the males for food. If there are too many of them, Pa will take more than one over the winter.

There are always a few deer living in our woodlot. It is important for Pa to keep the herd small so they will find enough wild grasses and acorns to eat and not eat much of our crops. Ma will preserve the meat and make sausage. Our relatives that live in the area receive fresh roasts and steaks. Fresh roast venison is always good!

I plunge into the woods and walk toward a ravine where I know the deer will be sheltered. There will be a good chance I will find them there and not have to estimate the number of animals by their tracks.

As I move along, I'm careful not to let an overhanging twig strike me in the face. It hurts something awful to have this happen on cold skin! I finally come across deer tracks and follow them along. They are leading me to the ravine for sure.

After quite a bit of walking, I see a group of deer ahead and try to move a little closer but something frightens them badly! What is it, I wonder. I'm being very quiet and the breeze is blowing away from the deer, not toward them so they couldn't have picked up my scent.

Suddenly I feel strange and ill at ease. Frightened is a better word! Stopping, I look all around me as Pa has told me to do. There is nothing unusual on my right, nothing wrong behind me. Then, over my left shoulder I see it! A cougar! A cougar is looking at me with its big yellow-green eyes!

The big cat is perched in a large oak tree on one of the lower limbs. It is much too close for comfort and what a surprise! The men have told us of occasionally seeing a big cat but I have never seen one before

The hair is standing up on the back of my neck and I'm suddenly very cold! An icy hand is gripping my throat! What should I do? If I run, the big cat might chase me and it would catch me in moments. I can't just stand here either. I can hear the deer running off. Perhaps the cougar will chase one of them.

I plan my route of escape, to my right. This will take me away from the cat and toward the edge of the woods where Pa, Doc, and Uncle Ed are working.

The cat turns to look at the deer and I take off at full speed. As fast as a foot of snow will let me run that is. After only a few steps, I trip over my big boots and fall face down into the snow!

Any moment the cat will be on me! I can almost feel it on my back! I'm afraid to look! Look I do. No cat! I get up and look some more. Still, no cat! Where is it? It couldn't have just disappeared. I have no answer to this question but am very thankful it isn't trying to catch me. Off I run. This time I run slower so I will not trip again.

Sure is strange the cat is not trying to catch me, as I cannot run nearly as fast as the deer. I bet Billy Marshall has never been this close to a cougar. The thought of this makes me feel good.

I come across my path into the woods and am able to make better time by following it. I'm not cold now. My breath is coming in huge gasps and my throat is burning from the cold air. Will I never get back to the area where my father and the men are working? Then, I see the stacks of logs.

"Pa, Pa," I holler as I burst into the open. He runs toward me, blue eyes sparkling, and grabs me up into his big arms. He is smiling and does not look concerned.

"What is the matter?" he asks.

I want to be calm and mature but all I can get out is a gasped, "Cat!"

We look in the direction I have come from. There is nothing there. Pa puts me down and asks, "What did you see?"

By this time, Doc and Uncle Ed have run to where we are standing. Pa repeats, "What did you see?"

I have calmed down a little bit and am getting my breath but I still gasp, "A cat! I saw a cougar who was stalking the deer herd! It ran off chasing a deer, I guess, and I ran back here."

No need to tell them that I had fallen for it was very evident because I have snow all down my front. Some has gone down the neck of my coat and is melting into my under drawers and wool shirts. It is up my sleeves too. I'm starting to shiver in spite of my running efforts.

Pa calls to Uncle Ed, "Ed, follow his track for a way and make sure the cat isn't nearby."

Uncle Ed starts out at a fast walk, his head is up, and he is carefully looking in all directions. I can see Pa looking at the team. They will know if a cat is nearby and will show it. The horses are quiet but looking our way, ears pointed toward us, as if to check out what the fuss is about.

Pa says to Doc, "Let's get these final logs on the bob so we can get out of here when Ed comes back. It looks like it might start to snow anyway."

I hadn't noticed the sky is getting quite dark off to the northwest and the wind has begun to blow. Shortly Uncle Ed appears out of the woods. "No sign of the cat, it must have followed the deer," he says.

Boy, am I relieved!

The men finish loading the bobsled. The logs are stacked all the way to the top of the rack.

"Danny, please go get the team," Pa says.

"Yes, Pa." I'm glad to have something to do because I'm getting quite cold just standing around. The horses watch me walk toward them but I speak to them anyway.

"Hello Kit, hello Bess, we are going home." They eye me carefully, hoping I have another treat for them. I pat them on the nose and whisper, "It's back to the barn and some hay for you two."

Kit nudges me with her big head and knocks me off my feet. I was somewhat ready for this because she does it quite often, even to the men. Of course, it does not knock them off their feet as it did me. Will I never grow any bigger and stronger?

I pick myself up and can hear Uncle Ed laughing at me. I give him my best grin.

After untying their lead lines, I carefully turn the team around. We walk slowly toward the bobsled. Then I judge just the right spot, turn the team, and guide them back toward the tongue of the sled as I have seen the men do.

"Back, Bess, back Kit. Whoa." The team is in the right position so hitching them to the sled will be easy.

I look at Pa for some sign of approval but he says nothing. I know though, by the look on his face, he is pleased. As Doc walks behind me to make the hitch, he gives me a slap on the back. This is all the recognition I need.

By this time, all of us have very red faces from the cold. Doc has frost in his moustache from his breath freezing there. My fingers are painfully cold in spite of having them made into fists inside my mittens most of the time.

Pa carefully places me in the center of Bess' back. I give her a hug and am thankful to be sitting on something so warm.

The men sit on the logs, even Pa, who is driving the team. There is no need to stand because the pile makes him high enough to be able to see over the backs of the horses.

I hear him make his clucking sound and call, "Giddyap Kit, Giddyap Bess."

The team lean into their harness and after some effort we are under way.

Soon Pa shouts, "Low bridge," as the horses walk under an oak tree branch. This is for my benefit in case I had not seen it. I lay flat on Bess' back and the branch misses me by inches. Pa is grinning at me as I look back at him his blue eyes are shining. Then I know he had directed the horses under the tree limb on purpose. The men on the pile of logs had to duck too. They are laughing at me, as I lay flat on Bess' broad back.

We follow our path back down the lane, and through the old corn and bean fields. The wind is drifting the snow in some places and our old track is gone but the horses need no guidance or urging to go to their stalls.

It is starting to snow in the little flakes of very cold weather. In spite of the heavy load, the horses seem to be moving a little faster than they did when we were going to the woodlot. They know there will be lots of hay for them to eat when they return to their stalls.

Pa guides the team to the windmill house where the logs will be cut into firewood with the buzz saw. This work is for after dinner. Doc and Uncle Ed jump off the load while Pa helps me down from Bess.

"Are you warmed up now?" he asks.

"I'm fine, do you want me to help put the team away and water them?" I reply.

"Work with your Uncle," Pa directs.

I'm thrilled to have another job to do. Pa hadn't sent me to the house where Ma would fuss over me. She won't like my being wet.

Doc and Uncle Ed have guided the team so that the sled is next to the mill house. The back end of the sled is close to the saw bed near the tackle used to lift the biggest logs into position.

Uncle Ed and I unhitch the team and let them walk slowly toward their barn. They need no guidance from us. Uncle Ed rolls open the big door with little effort. I still cannot budge it try as I might. UGH! Someday, I think to myself, I will be able to open this door.

We remove the harness from first Kit and then Bess and let them go to the watering trough. I pump more water for them. The barn beams have large wooden pegs to hang the harness on. I'm not much help here. It is impossible for me to hang up the horse collars. They are too big and heavy. The rest of the harness I drag under the pegs. I can't even reach them.

Uncle Ed, smiling, says, "Here, I'll do that."

"Thanks, Uncle Ed," I reply. "I wish I would grow some."

"You will, Danny. One day you will just sprout up like a weed. I was about your age when I started to grow tall. Be patient and the time will come."

While the horses are noisily drinking, Uncle Ed asks, "How big was the cougar?"

"Seemed very big to me," I reply. "He looked right at me with those big yellow eyes. Boy, I'm glad he was more interested in the deer than me. I was really scared."

"It was the right time to be scared. Coming across a big cat like that in the woods is something to be scared about. Cats are very unpredictable. Just think of the strange things Clara does sometimes. In this case you should have been quite safe because the cat was sure deer was food, he was not so sure about you," Uncle Ed laughs. "Still, he could have wanted to get you." He is serious again.

After finishing drinking and without any help from us, the horses walk into their box stalls.

"I'll get some hay." Hay is waiting for them in their mangers but I put in some more. Doc or Uncle Ed had pitched down a pile onto the barn floor from the haymow this morning.

"You boys ready for dinner?" Pa calls into the barn.

"You bet," we reply. It seems like forever since I had eaten breakfast.

Ma had watched us slowly make our way from the woodlot and across the fields to the barnyard. She has dinner all ready for us to enjoy. We take off our boots, brush off the snow from our coats and pants in the wood-shed, and enter the kitchen. The room is nice and warm and sure smells good. The comfort of it is enough to make me forget about my excitement in the woods. Well, almost forget.

I struggle out of my outer layers of clothing and Ma sees that I'm wet. The men hang their coats and hats on hooks next to the door and wash their hands.

"What happened to you?" she asks in her best concerned voice.

"I was running and I tripped over my big boots and fell in the snow," I tell her as I hang up my things on one of the lower hooks.

Ma continues with, "What were you doing running in the woods?"

Pa comes to my rescue with, "Let's eat, we can hear about Danny's adventure later. We are cold and hungry."

"Danny has to have dry clothes before he can eat!" Ma exclaims. "Go up to your room after you wash and change. You will have to use your flannel shirts."

"Can't I eat first? I'm starving."

"No, wash up and get into warm, dry clothes I said. I don't want to see you shivering needlessly."

"Yes, Ma," I wash and run up the back stairs to my room.

Ruthie had picked-up on Pa saying I had an adventure and I could hear her loudly ask, "What adventure? What did he do?"

I know she couldn't stand it to have to wait to find out what happened. It makes me feel good to make her wait. We get along quite well as brother and sister but sometimes she picks on me something awful. Now is my chance to get back at her. So, I take my time getting out of the wet shirts, putting them where they will dry and finding and putting on the flannel ones.

I can hear her ask what is taking me so long. Then she hollers up the stairs, "Danny, where are you? What adventure did you have?"

"Hold your horses, I'll be there in a minute," I shout. I walk down the stairs rather then run. When I get back to the kitchen, everyone is sitting at the dining table except Ma and Ruthie and I realize I have kept my family waiting. I feel ashamed and know my face has become a little red.

"Sorry I took so long," I mutter. Ma is putting food in big serving dishes while Ruthie is placing them at the head of the table where Pa is sitting.

"What adventure?" Ruthie asks again, her voice filled with obvious curiosity. "Will you sit and tell us?"

"Please pass the bread, Sis," Pa says. He often calls Mary, Sis. He is piling food on his plate and passing the dishes along to the others. Mary is carefully helping Carolyn by cutting her meat into small pieces.

Ma had baked bread while we were at the woodlot. We have it to eat, warm from the oven. Yum!

"Go ahead, Danny, tell Ma about your walk in the woods," Pa instructs as I sit at my place at the table.

"Well, I walked over toward the ravine to see if I could find the deer herd to learn their condition and about how many there are. I found their track leading to the ravine all right and followed it along. Sure enough, there was the herd in that place that is mostly clear of trees but has high banks around it. You know where I mean don't you?" Ma and Ruthie nod. Ruthie looks at me with displeasure. She is in a hurry to find out what happened.

"You mean where we sometimes have a picnic?" Mary asks.

"Yes, that is the place."

"Well, I was trying to count them when they suddenly spooked and started to run off. I looked around to see if I could find why and saw a big cougar."

I look at the girls to see their expressions. They all look astonished and concerned, even Ruthie. Mary's mouth is wide open and her eyes show fear. I feel brave and like a big brother.

"A cougar!" Ma says. "Oh Charles!" she exclaims.

"Not to worry, Ellen. The cat was more interested in the deer than any human," Pa explains.

Uncle Ed looks at me and nods in a knowing way.

I feel like a real man because all the girls are looking at me in amazement. I try to look indifferent. "That is right; the cat just stared at me and chased after the deer when they ran. The condition of the deer looks good, Pa and there seem to be several bucks too," I continue.

Carolyn exclaims, "Cat, cat, cat, why all the talk about a cat? We have lots of them right here at home. Clara is right over there!" Clara is asleep under an unused chair; it is a safe place to keep someone from stepping on her.

"Be quiet, Carolyn," Mary orders, "This is a different kind of cat. It is a big cat, one that can eat you."

Carolyn lets out a wail, "I don't want a cat to eat me!"

"Mary, now you be quiet," Ma says. "Don't scare her. Everything is all right, Little One, we are not talking about our pet cats. We are talking about a big wild cat that lives in the woods," Ma speaks softly to the little girl. She gives her a little pat on her cheek to help her feel secure.

Carolyn squeaks, "Oh, all right then," blinking back tears. She doesn't look convinced.

"When I go to hunt deer in a few days, I will have a good look around. I just hope the cat doesn't scare off the herd," Pa states in his matter of fact way. "If the cat is still around, I may have to shoot it. I can't have it eating all the deer for it will start to kill our livestock next. We need some of the deer for family use this winter."

"What else did you do while the men got the logs?" Ruthie asks smugly.

"I took care of Kit and Bess," I say as if it was an everyday event.

"Oh pooh." Ruthie says. "That is nothing exciting."

Ruthie has been able to handle the horses for sometime now. She always gets to do things before I do. I want to yell at her and say, you always get to do stuff first. But, I know Ma and Pa would not like my yelling at my sister, especially at the dinner table. She had already done enough shouting for both of us anyway.

Everyone except Carolyn, who is cleaning her plate, has finished eating. We are waiting for desert. I don't ask for it, as only when everyone has finished eating will desert be offered.

"You may get your cookies now Ruthie," Ma directs. "Mary, you pour the milk, I'll get the coffee. Ruthie baked the cookies this morning," Ma continues.

"Oh pooh yourself," I say. "Anyone can bake cookies."

"Anyone can handle a team of horses," Ruthie yells. "When have you ever baked cookies?"

"Enough!" Pa exclaims as he scowls at us. "You both did good work. The molasses cookies are perfect, Ruthie. Just the way I like them, nice and thick and chewy."

"Thank you, Pa," replies Ruthie with her 'I won' look on her face.

"You children can leave the table when you have finished your milk and cookies," Ma instructs.

I know she wants to talk to Pa about the deer and the big cat problem. She does not want us children to listen to the talk of killing it.

I don't want the big cat killed but know it is a matter of protecting one of our food sources and our livestock. And us!

"You boys get started out there. I will join you in a few minutes," Pa says. "Danny, you can stack for us and make kindling. That will be a big help."

"Yes, Pa."

Doc speaks for himself and Uncle Ed when he says, "Dinner was excellent, as always, Misses. The cookies are good too, Ruth." Beneath his gray moustache, he is grinning. Uncle Ed nods and smiles in agreement, as he tries to straighten his rumpled hair. Ruthie beams and Ma acknowledges his compliment with a sparkling smile.

CHAPTER 3

▼

THE BUZZ SAW

Doc, Uncle Ed, and I put on our warm outer clothes once again. My cotton flannel shirts will not be as warm as the wool ones. However, they are the only other winter shirts I have and I'm thankful for them.

The three of us plunge outdoors into the wind and snow. The wind is blowing quite hard out of the northwest and the air feels more frigid than it did this morning.

"It is just the right wind for using the windmill to drive the saw," Doc says. "We will make short work of these logs."

Yes, with Danny to help, this will go real fast," Uncle says with a laugh.

"Oh, thanks a lot," I say. "I won't get to do anything but stack. But that is better than nothing."

"Every bit helps, Danny," Doc says. "And you are a good help too."

"Thanks." I'm grateful he values my small contribution.

Pa and Doc had gotten the windmill ready to power the big saw while Uncle Ed and I put the team away. In order for the buzz saw to be effective there has to be lots of wind to drive the windmill fast enough to turn the saw with enough speed and power to cut the logs.

I get the hand sled and the splitting maul and stand out of the wind and out of the men's way.

Pa is in the mill building now and walks over to the lever that controls the power to the saw. When he is satisfied, all are in a safe spot he nods to Doc who is standing at the base of the tower that holds the windmill. He pulls the rope that connects to the mechanism at the top. This turns the blades so they will catch the wind and the whole assembly begins to rotate. Faster and faster, it goes with a loud whirring sound.

Pa pushes the big lever forward and connects the windmill's power to the saw blade. I can hear the whine of the rotating saw and Pa again nods to Doc. Doc and Uncle Ed move the first log so the saw teeth will begin to cut it. Stove length pieces are cut one by one.

The splitting of the wood is done by hand with a splitting maul. Pa and Uncle Ed work on this part of the project while Doc and I carry the wood into the woodshed and stack it. I get to wear leather gloves now too for my mittens will not stand up to the sharp bark of the wood. The gloves are much too big for me but they do the job of protecting my hands.

For use in the cookstove, some wood is split into even smaller pieces. It is much easier to control the amount of heat with small pieces.

One of my jobs is to split very small pieces of wood for kindling. This duty had been Ruthie's but last winter the job became mine. I find a place out of the wind and out of the way of the men and begin. Pa is watching me to see the care I'm taking not to get hurt. It will be very easy to cut my finger off if I'm careless. About a month ago, I did take a chunk out of the little finger of my left hand. This taught me a lesson for sure.

I carefully select the smaller pieces and split them into kindling using a small hatchet. I gather the wood into several large bushel baskets for the men to lug into the woodshed.

We continue all afternoon with this work. I'm getting tired but do not say anything about it. I do not want the men to think I'm a sissy. There is no worry about being cold that is for sure.

About mid afternoon, Ruthie comes out with steaming hot cups of tea and some cookies. It is good to stop work for a few minutes.

"Hello everyone, how is the work going? You must be getting tired by now aren't you little brother?" Ruthie's coat, hood, and boots cover her from head to toe.

"I'm not tired one bit," I reply loudly. "Thanks for the goodies."

"Did you split all the kindling?" Ruthie asks.

"Sure did," I reply proudly.

"Looks like some of the pieces are too big. Ma likes them small you know."

"Now Ruthie, do you always have to tell me how to do stuff? Ma hasn't complained about my kindling."

Uncle Ed comes over to my side to give me some moral support. He has already eaten his cookies and is noisily slurping his tea.

"He is doing a good job, Ruth and is keeping us entertained with his efforts."

"Boy, I'm being picked on from two sides now," I say. "I have to wear these huge gloves that fall right off my hands. I don't have giant hands like my big sister does." I'm slurping my tea quickly too, before it cools off in the cold air as snowflakes disappear into it.

"Well, if you weren't such a little runt you wouldn't have so much trouble doing work around the place."

"Ruth!" I hear Pa holler, "That is enough. He is doing a good job so stop picking on him."

Ruthie laughs and runs for the house.

The wood for use in the cookstove is stacked at the end of the wood-shed that is closest to the kitchen door. The wood to heat the house is stacked at the far end of the woodshed.

We finish work and Pa stops the buzz saw by pulling the lever toward him. Doc feathers the windmill and all is quiet again except for the wind howling around the mill house.

Pa asks Doc, "How much room do we have left in the shed?"

Doc replies, "About one third."

"Good," Pa says, "We will get another load on Monday and take some of it to Uncle Jerome and Aunt Liz. They will be getting quite low by now."

I hope the trip to Uncle Jerome's place will be left until I get home from school. I love to hear him talk about his War of the Rebellion experiences. "May I go to Uncle Jerome's place with you?"

"You have to go to school," Pa answers, "And I don't know when we will be going there. We will be without our helper and it will take us longer to get a load ready. Perhaps you can meet us there after school. We'll see."

I know he is teasing me about being a help. There is much work to do, and I want to be a help when I can. I am the only boy in our family and want to do my part.

Ruthie comes out of the woodshed door. She is bundled up to keep out the cold and has a basket with her. Ruthie is going to gather the eggs and feed the chickens and turkeys. My big sister and I take turns taking care of the chickens, turkeys, horses, and pigs. It is my week to do the pigs and horses.

"It is getting to be supper time, Danny, go do your pig and horse chores," she says.

Ruthie likes bossing me around and sometimes she makes me angry, telling me what to do as if she is Ma or Pa.

"Ha ha, you have to do the pigs! Don't take too long. You are such a slowpoke."

Yes, I know it is my turn to do the pigs and horses," I say with impatience. "I'll do it as soon as I finish here. Why do you only have stuff to say to me when you want to boss me around? I have been working hard all afternoon what have you been doing?"

"It is none of your business what I have been doing," Ruthie replies giving me a cold look. "You need telling when and what to do. And that is the only time you are worth talking to." She walks away quickly.

The pigs live in the basement of the horse barn in the winter. The females have a small outside yard they can use if they want during the day. At this time, we have one boar or male pig and four sows or female pigs.

We keep Berkshires. They are black in color with white on the feet, face and tail tip. They have a short upturned nose and long body. They are excellent for meat.

I go to the back door of the house and Ma gives me a pail with vegetable skins and other scraps from the kitchen in it. It is starting to get dark now as I walk to the door that goes to the horse barn basement. A little light filters in through the barn windows. I dump the slop into the trough in each of the two pens and the pigs noisily gobble it up.

Then I go up the stairs to the granary to get a pail of pig mash and a few ears of dried corn. While I'm upstairs, I give each horse a big pail of water and some hay and clean up their manure. This I throw out the door onto the manure pile in the barnyard. If a stall needs fresh straw, I add some. The straw absorbs the liquid and makes clean up easier.

In addition to the two teams of draft horses, we have a team of light duty horses. These are dapple gray and very beautiful. Dapple gray means the horses are light gray in color with dark gray round spots mostly on their legs and hindquarters. These horses are to be ridden or used with a light wagon, cart, or sleigh.

One of the men grooms the horses each day, usually in the morning. Ruthie and I want to do this chore and she does help sometimes. I'm just too short to be of much help.

Back down stairs, I give some of the corn and mash to the boar, and the rest to the sows. Then I make another trip upstairs to get two pails of water for the pigs. I enter each pen and shovel up the manure. Pigs are clean animals, always soiling only one area of the pen. This straw-manure mixture I put into a big two-wheeled cart the men will empty onto the outside manure pile when it is full. I pitch around some fresh straw.

The animals pay no attention to me as I work. They are too busy eating. My, they make a lot of noise and the oldest sow always tries to grab the most food. I make sure all the pigs are in their pens and lock them in for the night.

Mostly we do not name the pigs because they usually do not stay with us very long. They are for making money. When baby pigs reach six weeks old, they are sold. By this time, the babies are weaned from their mother's milk. People buy them to raise until they are big enough to slaughter for meat. Butchering is done when the little pigs reach five to eleven months of age depending on how much the pig weighs.

Some of the babies we keep to raise and butcher for our own use or to sell the meat and hides. We children all hate slaughtering time but Pa needs cash money so he can buy the things our family does not raise or produce.

It is not a good idea for us children to make pets out of the baby pigs. We have strict orders not to take the death or sale of an animal personally. They are our friends but farm animals die or are sold, it is a common thing—part of farm life.

We use different ways to tell the pigs apart by using some kind of mark they have. One has a wrinkled ear and another has no white spot on her tail.

My barn chores are finished and back into the house I go. Pa, Doc, and Uncle Ed are doing the other routine night chores such as milking, watering, and feeding the dairy cows, feeding, and watering the beef cows.

In the summer when the men have many other farm related things to do and I'm not in school, I help with this work. Ruthie does some of this work too when she is not helping Ma in the house or with the garden. She and I hope Mary will be helping soon. She will start working with the chickens and turkeys just as Ruthie and I had. Then I will have someone to boss around and different work to do. I'm sure Mary will learn fast.

Mary's job now, besides helping Ma with housework and Carolyn, is to feed Clara some milk and a little bit of meat. We do not want to feed the cat well because she needs to be willing to hunt for mice in the house.

After supper, all we children except Carolyn help clean up the kitchen. I resent having to do this women's work but know there is no use complaining about it. I'll move onto something better soon.

While we are doing the kitchen work, Pa, Doc, and Uncle Ed normally discuss their work for the next day. Since the next day is Sunday, Doc and Uncle Ed stay in the family parlor only as long as we children are working in the kitchen. They then say, "good night" and go upstairs to their rooms to play cards, talk, and go to sleep after a long day.

When Ma and we children come into the room, Pa reaches for the book he is reading to us. Comforting warmth is coming from the parlor stove as Pa recently added wood to it.

This is by far one of my favorite times of the day, when Pa reads aloud to us, he uses his best dramatic voice. He is reading *Kidnapped* by Robert Louis Stevenson and although we have heard it several times, we look forward to it each evening. The book is part of a neighborhood circulating library. Books are treasured and are passed from family to family to be read and reread. Pa turns up the oil lamp and by its soft glow pretends to concentrate hard.

"Does anyone know where I left off last night? I can't find my place," he says as he leafs through the pages.

Ruthie and I know he is teasing us. Mary, as usual, doesn't understand and chirps up with, "You were going to read the part about Davie meeting his Uncle Ebenezer Balfour." She becomes red in the face when we laugh. "Oh, you were teasing me," she cries. "No fair."

"You are fun to tease, Sis, as you take things so seriously. You are right as two rabbits. That is where we stopped last time. Is everyone settled? Shall I begin?" Pa asks.

"Pa, are you going to shoot the cougar?" I ask.

"I hope I don't have to. However, if we see it around close to the house, I will. It might become so bold as to come right into the barnyard."

"Wow! That would be something, wouldn't it?" I ask.

"Yes, but I would rather it didn't happen. I want the cougar alive and living free in the woods but he could put all of us in danger."

Sometimes, if I have a lot of schoolwork to do, I miss Pa's reading aloud. Schoolwork is more important.

After Pa reads for about an hour, he puts the book away and we all know it is time to go to bed. Pa gives us each a hug, Ma kisses us a loving good night and we all wish each other sleep tight. Carolyn has long since fallen to sleep on Ma's lap and is carried up stairs and put to bed.

Ma goes to the kitchen to bank the fire in the cookstove and Pa does the same in the parlor stove. By piling up the ashes over the coals, the fire will burn longer. Pa will get up during the night and put more wood on both fires tonight because it is very cold and windy.

My bedroom is cold and I undress as quickly as I can. I put on my flannel nightshirt over my under drawers and jump into bed. Ma has given me a brick heated in the oven of the cookstove and wrapped in an old towel for my feet. Flannel sheets help a lot and I warm up quickly.

I try to go to sleep but sleep will not come. I get up and wrap myself in a quilt, light my candle, and huddle by the register that comes into my room. It is not giving off much heat but is better than nothing. I try to read my Fourth Grade McGuffey Reader but just can't get comfortable enough.

The wind is rattling my windows and howling about the corner of the house.

Back into bed, I crawl and squirm further under the blankets but still don't go to sleep. The cougar adventure keeps entering my head. I wonder if the cat had thought about catching me. My body shivers when I think of that possibility.

I worry about the big cat and wonder if Pa will kill it in a few days. It is a beautiful animal! Perhaps he will not be able to find it when he goes hunting. I don't want the cat to kill the deer either but I know that is its nature. Finally, I fall to sleep.

CHAPTER 4

▼

SUNDAY

Time to get up comes early on a farm; even on Sunday, there are always routine chores that need doing. I can hear Ma shaking the ashes out of the grate in the cookstove to get it ready to make breakfast. I heard Pa remove the ashes from the parlor stove and add more wood sometime ago.

The girls are talking and giggling in their room so I know they will be downstairs soon. I had better get a move on if I'm to beat Ruthie. My big sister doesn't need another opening to tell me to go do my chores.

I dress as quickly as I can in my very cold room and run down the back stairs to the kitchen. Ma is making the dough for the sweet buns we are going to have for breakfast. She is at the small table in the kitchen where she does most of her cooking and is humming, as is her way while doing her work.

"Good morning, Ma, do you need more wood? Do the ashes need taking out?"

"Good morning to you Danny. No, thanks, I have enough for now and the ash bin is only half full," she replies. "Did you sleep well?"

"No, I kept thinking about the cougar. I hope it goes away so Pa doesn't have to shoot it."

Ma gives me a hug and says, "Yes, I agree, I don't want him to have to go near it. Be sure and dress really warm when you go to the barn for it is very cold."

"Yes'm, I will," I say with a smile for I knew she was going to say this.

Pa, Doc, and Uncle Ed are already out in the cow barn. The beef and dairy cows live together in the basement. The upstairs stores the hay, corn stalks, and grain we feed the cows for the winter.

Doc and Uncle Ed do not do any work on Sunday, just as we don't, other than the everyday chores of taking care of the livestock. The farm animals have to be cared for every day, no matter what. Sometimes, in good weather, Doc goes to his daughter's home in Penn Yan on Saturday afternoon in the winter. This means Pa and Uncle Ed have extra to do. Ruthie and I help with what we can.

I stand by the cookstove for a few minutes to warm myself before going to the horse barn. The stove is nice and warm and soon breakfast will be cooking on it. Then I hear Ruthie in the upstairs hall.

"I'm going out to do my chores, Ma," I say as I put on my winter coat, hat, and mittens. "Did you see the ice on the trees? Isn't it dazzling with the sun shining like that?"

"Yes, I admired it when I came into the kitchen. I can never see enough of the sunrise on the snow. Earlier it was all pink and orange and sparkly. Now don't dawdle, the men have been to work for sometime now and will want their breakfast when they come in," she says.

"Hello Buster," I call as I run out the back door and jump into my boots in the woodshed. Wow, they are cold!

Buster greets me with his usual jumping and tail wagging. "How are you this fine morning? Were you warm enough last night? I wish you could sleep with me in my bed. We could keep each other warm." Buster replies by licking my face while I give him a big hug.

There has been more snow during the night and I find the walking to the horse barn to be difficult. After kicking the snow away from the basement door, I go inside and am glad to be out of the cold. The presence of the pigs and being out of the wind makes the barn seem warm. It takes a few moments for my eyes to adjust to the darkness so I just stand still taking in the noises and smells.

The pigs are grunting, snorting and oinking me their greetings. In a moment, I can see that they are all right in their pens and are looking my way hoping I have something for them to eat.

"Sorry Mr. Pig and Mrs. Pigs, no food for you now. I'll give you some tonight," I say as if they can understand what I'm telling them. I fill their water pails from the trough upstairs. There is no ice yet. The heat from the horses' bodies is keeping the water from freezing.

After cleaning up their manure and putting down new straw, I'm finished with the pigs. Back up stairs, I go to take care of the horses.

First, I speak to each one and give it a few pats on the nose. The men have already been here to groom them. Someday I will be able to groom them. Each horse gets their usual amount of oats; the draft horses about two quarts each because they will not be doing any work today. The two grays each receive about two quarts of oats because they will be pulling the large family cutter when we go to Sunday school. Then I give the horses a big pitchfork full of hay in their manger. This is the easy part. Now I have to give them water, about four gallons per horse. I rest a few minutes and talk to Bess, my favorite, before cleaning out the manure.

"Good morning, Bess. Are you well this morning?" Bess answers by softly nickering. "Are you rested from your work?" I give her an extra wad of hay from my hand and watch her chewing away.

Now it is time for my breakfast. Quickly I run down the stairs and out the basement door. The frigid wind is blowing the snow right into my face as I run to the house. Boy, am I glad to be in the woodshed! I pull off my boots and put them in their place; it is now I realize all the other boots are in their places. Everyone is waiting for me, again.

"Good morning, everyone," I begin. Before I can say anything else, Ruthie brags about beating me.

"Slow poke, slow poke," she taunts, "What took you so long? We have been waiting for you forever."

Ma takes pity on me and says, "Never mind, Ruthie, wash up and sit to the table Danny, breakfast is ready."

"Sorry I took so long, some of us try to do a very good job when it comes to chores, Ruthie," I reply. She always does a good job even though I don't want to admit it.

"Are you suggesting I don't do a good job with my chores? I'm just faster than you are, that's all. You will get done sooner if you didn't stop to talk to the animals."

"But I want to talk to them. I like them and they are my friends."

"It is silly to talk to them. They can't answer you, can they?"

"Well no, not really, but I like to think they can."

"Oh, how cute," Ruthie snickers.

"Better be quiet, Ruthie, it seems I have heard you talking to the chickens," Ma laughs.

"Please pass the butter," Pa requests of Ruthie. Ma and Ruthie had made a new batch of butter Saturday afternoon while we men were cutting and splitting the wood. They churned it by hand rather than using the large windmill-powered churn.

Ma prepared our usual Sunday breakfast of sweet rolls, applesauce, and ham and fried eggs. Butter is already inside the sweet rolls along with brown sugar and cinnamon. Yum! We children have hot chocolate too.

We are using the good dishes from the china cabinet in the dining room. These dishes belonged to my Grandmother Lee, my father's mother. Ma uses the dishes only on Sundays and holidays or when we have company. Grandma Lee's given name was Mary and my sister Mary was named for her.

The oak china cabinet belonged to Grandma Lee too. It is large and is fancy carved with curlicues, scrolls, and things that look like leaves. The top part has shelves for the dishes and the bottom part has doors and is where Ma keeps her tablecloths, napkins, and such.

Someday I would like to be able to make furniture as nice. My Pa is helping me to learn how to carve and make things out of wood.

Doc and Uncle Ed are eating with us too. Being Sunday, we children are on our best behavior.

"Are we going to Sunday school?" I ask.

"Yes, I'm heating your bath water right now," Ma replies, "It should be ready by the time you finish your breakfast."

Carolyn and Mary already had their baths before breakfast while the rest of us were doing chores. After breakfast is finished and the kitchen cleaned up, Pa puts the tub of warm water on the kitchen floor near the stove. He places a screen around it and first Ruthie and then I have a bath. Ma, Pa, Doc, and Uncle Ed had taken theirs last night after we children went to bed.

We only take a full bath once a week for it is a real chore. Water carried from the well outside the back door is poured into the tub. It takes quite a bit of time to heat the water on the cookstove. Water heated on the parlor stove is used for rinsing off.

It sure feels good to have that bath even if there are only a few inches of water in the tub. Ma has a large towel ready for me behind the screen and after I dry off and put on clean under drawers, I wrap up in a blanket for the trip upstairs.

My Ma is a picture of love and affection when we are taking our bathes in the winter. Not only do we need bath water that is the right temperature, we need to stay warm while drying off and getting our clothes on. She hovers about in the kitchen making sure things are just right.

We get dressed in our Sunday/party clothes. We children only have two dress-up outfits, summer and winter. Ruthie has a few more changes because she is learning to sew and mostly makes things for herself. Of course, Mary and Carolyn have hand-me-downs from Ruthie. I, being the only boy, get new things. I have a store-bought suit but Ma or Ruthie made my shirt and underdrawers.

The hardest part of all this activity is waiting while everyone gets ready. We men sit around in the parlor while the girls get into their dresses and have their hair fixed just right. I never can understand what the big deal is because their hair doesn't look much different then it does during the rest of the week. This extra effort does not change their behavior though. Ruthie is still bossy, Mary still innocent, and Carolyn is too young to know about anything. All that fuss for nothing. Girls!

My attention is on Clara who has found a spider on the parlor floor and is tracking it, ready to pounce. Shortly the poor spider is flat, under her right front paw. Clara's pressure is light so she can play with the eight-leg creature before killing it. Playing with spiders is one of her favorite pastimes. Sometimes she gets a little too rough and kills one before she means to and then she seems to have a disappointed look on her face. Then she eats it!

When the girls are finally ready, Pa, Doc, and Uncle Ed harness the grays and hitch them to the big family cutter. This sleigh Pa's father had built many years ago for his family. His name was Daniel and I'm named for him. He had died in 1884 when he fell from the horse barn roof then under construction. His wife, my Grandma Lee died a few months later from the shock of losing her husband.

I never knew either of them. Many times, I wonder what it would be like to have them with us. Would they like me?

While I'm on the subject of grandparents, I will tell you a little about my Mother's parents. Their family name is Scott. They live in the big stone Wagener Mansion. Mr. Wagener founded the town of Penn Yan in 1799 when he built the first house there. He also built this house.

That is how my Pa met my Ma because they were neighbors and fell in love and got married in the big stone house.

The cutter is a two seater with horsehide-upholstered seats. Pa had carefully repainted the cutter black with red trim last year. The sleigh is spiffy, but is wide, long, and difficult to maneuver.

The grays are tricky to handle too and only Pa or Doc seems to be able to make them behave when they are in harness. Their conduct is unreliable and they sometimes bolt for no apparent reason. Ma always is concerned whenever Toby and Andy are used. To explain this further Andy's full name is 'Wild Andy.'

The two of them are prancing and dancing in front of the cutter, steam coming from their nostrils. They are in high spirits.

"Steady, boys," Doc cries as he and Uncle Ed hold a horse's head while the rest of us climb into the sleigh, Ma with Carolyn on her lap, Ruthie, Mary, and I in the back. Pa, Doc, and Uncle Ed sit in the front seat. We have blankets over our laps and heated bricks at our feet to help keep us warm.

Mary is in the middle and asks for more room. "You two are taking up too much space. I'm being scrunched; move over."

"You will have to make do, we are at the end of our seats now," Ruthie says in a loud voice.

"Why am I always in the middle?" Mary whines.

"Because you are a girl," Ruthie says.

"If I'm a girl what are you?"

"I'm a young lady," Ruthie says with a smirk on her face.

"Poohie, you are just a large girl," I say. That gets her goat for sure. I get a scowl in return.

"Giddyap Toby, giddyap Andy," Pa commands with his deep voice, "Earn your keep for a change and behave yourselves." Off we move with a jingle and a jangle. The men have attached a leather strip of bells to each horse's harness. They make beautiful music that helps us forget how cold it is.

Sunday school meets in our schoolhouse, which is only about two and a half miles from home on the road to the lake. Our neighbors meet there because the area does not have a real church. There is no minister either. Community members elected Mr. Hicks to lead us in our Sunday school program. The meeting is very informal.

The horses slowly break their way through any drifts of snow we come across. Perhaps another six inches had fallen overnight. We can't leave the road as we had while going to the woodlot because there are vineyards on both sides. Snow covers the lower parts of the vines. Only the top few feet of the posts show where the snow has been blown into drifts.

The vines look forlorn in the cold without their leaves and being half-buried. They are beautiful in the growing season with their big green leaves with the deeply scalloped edges and the ripening fruit but now they are only a few gnarled stems and branches sticking above the snow.

"Charles, will we have trouble getting back up this hill?" Ma asks. "The snow seems awfully deep in places."

Pa calms her fears by remarking, "It is windy from the west so most of the snow should blow off the road. We shouldn't have any difficulty. Toby and Andy will get us through."

"Boy, I hope so," I say to myself. "I don't want to have to spend any extra time in the schoolhouse, during the week is quite enough."

As we pull into the schoolyard, I see that Uncle Henry's cutter is already there. Pa directs Toby and Andy so they will be next to Uncle Henry's team of blacks. One has a white area on his right hind leg and a white blaze on his face. Uncle Henry's team doesn't misbehave like Toby and Wild Andy.

We climb out of the sleigh and Doc and Uncle Ed put a blanket on each horse. They are securely tied to the hitching rail. We will not be here very long but the horses will appreciate the cover. It is dangerous to let a heated horse cool off too quickly. Uncle Henry has covered his horses too.

We all troop into the schoolhouse and sit in the back on the only remaining seats. There are about a dozen adult people there and some children.

Adults have a hard time squeezing themselves into the seats, which are attached to the floor. They are made of varnished wood with black iron legs and feet. The seat is part of the desk behind. There are grooves in the top of the desk for our chalk, pencil, and pen and a shelf underneath for our slate and books. There is also a hole in the desktop right corner for our ink well.

Our teacher has a desk, on a raised platform, in the front center of the room. A stove is in the center of the room but there hasn't been a fire in it very long so the room isn't very warm. We all leave our coats on. Mr. Hicks is standing behind the teacher's desk and is getting ready to speak. We are just in time.

Uncle Henry and his four children are there in the schoolroom but Aunt Mertie isn't. We are going to their house for Sunday dinner and she has stayed behind to get things ready.

I let my mind wander as Mr. Hicks is speaking. He is reading a passage from the Bible but I'm thinking about what we might have for dinner. Aunt Mertie is a good cook as is my Ma. After we have dinner there will be sliding down hill with my cousin, Jay.

Ma gives me a poke in the arm and glares at me. She knows I'm not paying attention to Mr. Hicks. After Ma's reminder I give what he is saying more heed after all it is only a few weeks to Christmas!

After Mr. Hicks finishes, we stand around and chat with neighbors we don't see much of in the winter.

Dinner at Uncle Henry's includes Doc who is like family. He had worked for Grandpa Lee when he first came to Bluff Point. Pa and Uncle Henry and Uncle Ed have known him almost all their lives.

It is nice to have family so close. Uncle Henry is also a brother of Pa's and is two years younger. I'm glad to go to Uncle Henry's farm because I will have his son Jay to do things with and will not have to hang around the girls and small children.

As we are getting into the cutter, I ask Pa, "May I get my sled when we stop at the house? Then I can slide down hill with Jay."

"Sure, Son," Pa replies, "Be sure to get a length of rope so we can tow the sled behind. There is no room to put it in the cutter. I think there is some hanging in the woodshed."

"Thanks, Pa."

The grays have no difficulty pulling the cutter back up the steep hill. Pa was right about the new snow, having been blown off.

"Get a pair of everyday pants and your old coat, hat, and boots," Ma reminds me as we pull up behind the house. "You can't slide down hill in your good clothes."

"Yes, Ma."

Ruthie and Mary chime in together, "And please hurry, it is cold sitting here."

I quickly jump out of the cutter and race toward the house.

Ma calls after me, "Get the rolls and two apple pies I baked yesterday, also a pound of butter."

"Yes, I will," I holler.

What am I going to put the rolls and pies in to carry them? I ask myself. The rolls already are in the breadbox so why not put the pie and butter in there too? I get the pies off the shelf and the butter out of the icebox. Carefully I put the rolls aside; there is just room for the pies in the bottom. After replacing the rolls, I put the butter on top and close the lid. It looks good to me. I run out of the house and give the breadbox to Ruthie to hold on her lap while I run to get my old clothes and some rope.

When I come out, Ruthie is looking in the breadbox and I know she is going to find fault with something.

"Just look at the way he put the butter and rolls on top of the pie, I'll bet the pie is ruined! Isn't that so, Ma?" she says in a loud voice for all to hear.

Ma, always the calming force, says, "Well, I think it will be all-right but it would have been better if you put the butter and rolls in another container, you must not have heard me tell you that. And Ruth, must you always be so critical of your brother?"

"Well, he always seems to do so many dumb things. He is a silly goose," she blurts out.

I was in a hurry so you will not have to sit out in the cold," I retort. "I do not always do dumb things." My teeth are set in anger.

"Children, it is Sunday, let's have some peace and quiet," Ma says in her hushed way.

I don't say anything more just look thankfully at Ma. Off to Uncle Henry's we go my sled in tow. His farm is north on the Ridge Road about a mile and then about half a mile over the ridge down toward the west branch of the lake.

It is a cold and windy trip but Andy and Toby have no trouble getting through. What snow there is, swirls around their legs as they trot along.

Uncle Henry comes out the kitchen door as we arrive. "You can put your team in the barn, Charlie," he instructs as we pull up to the house. "That sure is a nasty wind."

"I'll put your sled by the woodshed door, Danny," Uncle Ed says.

"Thanks a lot," I holler as I walk toward the house.

Pa's brothers and Uncle Jerome are the only ones to call Pa, Charlie. Everyone else calls him Charles. Just why that is, I'm not sure.

Uncle Henry looks a lot like my Pa except he isn't quite as tall and he has a full beard trimmed short. The beard and his hair are very dark as are his eyes. I cannot understand why he doesn't have blue eyes like my Pa. He seems a little gruff to Ruthie and me but perhaps it is just his dark beard, hair, and eyes.

Doc and Uncle Ed go to take care of the team and I carefully carry the breadbox into the house, hoping the pie hasn't been crushed.

Jay meets me at the door and right away asks, "Did you bring your sled?"

"Sure did," I reply. "Aunt Mertie, Ma brought some rolls, butter, and apple pie. I hope the pie is all right, I might have crushed it some," I tell her meekly.

"It will taste just as good even if it is a little busted, Danny," she tells me.

I like Aunt Mertie because she always seems easy going. She is short and quite round and keeps her dark hair neatly in a bun at the nape of her neck. She and Uncle Henry let Jay, who is only a year and a half older than I am, do many things I'm not allowed to do. Of course, there is the point that he is much taller, bigger, and stronger than I am.

Jay is not the only child in the family. Uncle Henry and Aunt Mertie have a daughter Ada who is two years older than Ruthie is. They also have two small sons, Warren and Alderman. These children are our cousins.

The girls and Ma troop into the kitchen and exchange greetings along with offers to help with dinner.

"There are just the last minute things, Ellen," Aunt Mertie explains. "Thanks for bringing the rolls, butter, and pie. Go sit in the parlor and I will let you know when things are ready. Ruthie, will you please put the rolls and butter on the table. Dinner will be ready in a few minutes."

Jay and I go into one corner of the parlor, while Ma, Mary, and Ada admire the dining table and talk about dishes and silverware. Carolyn is placed on the floor of the parlor to play with Warren and Alderman whom we call Aldy.

Jay and I play with his locomotive that his father carved out of walnut for him. It is nice and looks just like the real ones I see in town. It has two pairs of big wheels in the back and two pairs of small wheels in the front. I hope to have one like it someday.

"Let's go sledding right after dinner," Jay says. "Ada and I were there yesterday and it was great. We have a good path made."

"Oh, boy, I can hardly wait. But, eating dinner comes first," I say with a smile.

"Jay, go call the men in from the barn, dinner is ready. I don't know what they are standing out there in the cold for anyway," Aunt Mertie adds.

Cousin Jay throws on his coat and hat and runs out to the barn. He returns in a minute with the men following along.

Ma, Aunt Mertie, and Cousin Ada place dinner on the table. We are having roast chicken, mashed potatoes and gravy, stuffing, preserved beets in some kind of sauce, rolls, and butter. Cousin Ada has made a bread pudding with raisins and we have my Ma's apple pie for desert.

Jay and I try to eat fast so we can go sliding even though we know we will not be able to leave the table until everyone finishes. Pa, Uncle Henry, Doc, and Uncle Ed have seconds of everything.

The men are discussing the snow conditions and that the winter wheat has enough protection from the cold. This crop, planted last fall, will not be harvested until this coming summer. Winter wheat depends on a layer of snow to act as insulation to keep the cold winter winds off and help keep the plants alive.

"I'll cut wood with you next week for Uncle Jerome," Uncle Henry says.

"Thanks, Henry, when do you want to do it?"

"Oh, Wednesday or Thursday, I guess," Uncle Henry replies.

"How are Uncle Jerome and Aunt Liz?" Aunt Mertie asks.

"Not doing too badly. He seems a little weak but holding his own. Aunt Liz is her usual pleasant self. We are going to take them a load of wood tomorrow."

"That sounds encouraging. Now if we have an easy winter and none of the old folks get seriously sick they will be doing well," Aunt Mertie adds.

Why don't they hurry up? I ask myself. "Oh, boy, Aunt Mertie, everything is so very good. I might as well have something more to eat. Another slice of chicken on a roll will go down very easily. Thank you for making dinner."

Ruthie adds, "You ate enough for two people, oink, oink!"

"I'm trying to grow tall like Jay and a person has to eat to do that, isn't that right, Pa?"

"That's right Danny, one of these days you will start to grow again, you are just resting right now." Everyone laughs but me. I seem to be the only one who is concerned about my height. It isn't funny for me to be so short. It is awful to be shorter than your little sister is!

Aunt Mertie says, "You are more than welcome, Danny. It is a pleasure to have some of the family together in weather like this. You boys can go sliding now; we girls will do the cleaning up."

I make my best bad face at Ruthie and stick out my tongue at her. For once, she didn't have a smart-aleck reply. She is at a loss for words.

"Come on, Jay, let's go."

We go to Jay's room and climb into our old clothes. I carefully place my good things on Jay's bed. We run down stairs, grab our outer duds, dash out the back door and to the woodshed where our boots and sleds are. I put on my too big boots and know they will make climbing up the hill difficult. It will be worth it to slide down the long hill behind Uncle Henry's house.

On the way up the hill, I tell Jay about the cougar. He listens in silence, mouth-hanging open. "Weren't you scared?" he asks.

"Nah," I boast but then quickly add, "Well, some."

"What is your Pa going to do, kill it?"

"I hope not, but he said he might if it kills too many deer or comes to our barnyard. That big cat sure is a beautiful animal."

"It is a good thing it didn't catch you!"

"Yup, I would have been a goner for sure!"

After fully discussing the cougar's chances, we are at the top of the long hill.

For my first run, I try to get a good fast start but, as usual, find I can't run well and make a bad beginning. I can hear Jay laughing as I slide down the hill.

He waits until I'm nearly all the way down and then hollers, "I'll show you how it should be done," he boasts. "Gang way, here I come!"

I get off my sled to watch him speed down the hill. He does a good job of doing a belly-whacker and manages to stay in the track all the way. I am really challenged now. My next ride has to be much better than the first.

"See if you can beat that one, Danny," Jay taunts in a good-natured way. We mark his stopping place with a big snowball and up the hill, we trudge.

"I will give you one more practice run before you are put to the test, after all fair is fair," Jay says.

I take up the challenge and say, "All right, one more practice run." After resting a moment when we get to the top of the hill, I get myself ready for the best belly-whacker of my life. I'm off to a good start but once again, my boots make running fast difficult. It is a good ride but my stopping point is not even close to Jay's.

"Here I come," Jay calls as he flops onto his sled.

I make sure I'm out of his way and watch him all the way down the hill. I don't see that he does anything differently than I did except that his starting run was much faster. He didn't do as well as the first time though. We trudge back up.

How am I going to do better? I ask myself. I don't need to win, just come close. I really need to do something well. I have it! I'll take off my boots and make my starting run without them! That is what I do. Jay must have thought I was crazy at first but he quickly catches onto what I'm doing.

"Good idea. I'll bring your boots down on my run," he says.

I run as hard as I can and make a perfect flop onto my sled and I'm off to a good start. Now all I have to do is stay in the track to not slow in the loose snow. My sled is moving so fast my eyes are watering but I manage to stay in the track by shifting my weight ever so slightly and using the steering handles on my sled only a little. I can't see the marked spot where the finish line is but when I coast to a stop I realize it is just two feet in front of me! I'm satisfied I have done the best I can.

"Yippee, yippee," I scream.

Jay hollers, "Stay on your sled, I'm bringing your boots."

My feet are becoming cold after being in the snow in spite of the felts and wool stockings. I sit up and quickly brush off the snow before it has a chance to melt. Jay comes down on an easy run and hands me my boots.

"Wow, good job! You see, it is just that your boots slow you down," he says as he hands them to me.

"Yeah, that run was much better but I don't want to do it again without my boots," I remark. I manage to get most of the snow off my stockings and felts and gratefully pull on the boots.

We continue to ride down hill until we realize it is starting to get dark. Dusk always comes too soon! We know we have to get to the house because my Pa will want to start for home and I still have to get my good clothes from Jay's room.

We get to the house just as Ma, Pa, and the girls are coming out. Ruthie has my clothes and I can see that Doc and Uncle Ed have the team and cutter ready. Jay and I aren't a minute too soon.

"Jay, remember to bring your skates when you come to our place, the ice pond is well frozen," I tell him.

"I will for sure!" Jay exclaims.

"Thanks for bringing my good clothes, Ruthie."

"If you weren't so late you could have gotten them yourself," she tells me in her big sister voice.

I wave good-byes to the rest of Uncle Henry's folks who are looking out at us through the kitchen windows and hurriedly tie my sled on behind the cutter.

CHAPTER 5

▼

THE RIDE HOME

It seems to be much colder now that I'm standing still. The sky is getting dark off to the west with the setting sun. We are making a late start for home. I hope Ma and Pa haven't been waiting for me. I feel somewhat ashamed and concerned that I'm responsible for this delay just so Jay and I could slide down hill one more time.

The sky is clear and the moon will be out soon so we will have some light to see the road by. Besides, the team and Pa have been over this road many times. There is nothing to worry about but I know Ma is distressed just the same. Ma does not like riding in the dark, as she does not trust this high-spirited team. She has often asked Pa why he bought them.

"Why Ellen, you know how beautiful they are and how much we all enjoy watching them move. And when we come to town with them people admire the team and tell me how splendid they are," is his answer.

"It seems a little prideful to me," Ma remarks.

"It well might be pride but the team is worth having pride for," Pa answers carefully.

We all pile into the sleigh as before. Doc and Uncle Ed again hold a horse's head until Pa is ready to control the team from the cutter.

Ma taps him on the shoulder and says, "Charles, please be extra careful! I'm concerned about the reliability of this team."

"Yes, I know you are but they have been behaving well of late." With his firm verbal commands and his touch on the reins, Pa urges the team into motion. Ma is holding Carolyn, and Mary has a bowl of bread pudding Aunt Mertie had given to us on her lap. Ruthie is holding my clothes. Little Carolyn is already asleep after a busy afternoon playing with her two cousins. I have the now empty breadbox.

Pa asks Toby and Andy to trot and the sleigh, in spite of its load, is moving quickly up the hill. The trees on either side of the lane are flying by and I know Ma is getting upset about our speed. It is also quite dark due to the closeness of the trees.

"Charles, we are going too fast!" she calls to him.

"Not to worry, Ellen, the team is well in control," Pa calls back to her. However, he slows them to a walk to calm her. We get up to where there are only trees on one side of the lane. On the right side, there is a hedgerow of trees and bushes. On the left is an open field, which last year had been planted to oats.

The moon is just coming up on the other side of the lake to the east. It is only about half full but gives some golden light. The snow is all sparkles like a thousand jewels. It is a beautiful sight out in the open as we are.

Pa again urges the horses into a trot. The cutter no more than gets moving fast when out of the trees on the right jumps a red fox. It runs across the lane under the noses of the team, and is gone in the semi-darkness.

Both Toby and Andy snort and rear onto their hind legs, ears held close to their heads, fore limbs thrashing the air! I can hear Ma and the girls scream and see Uncle Ed jump out and make a dash for the horse's heads. Too late! He misses grabbing hold of Andy's bridle by inches and the horse rears again! Pa hands the reins to Doc and leaps from the cutter. Both horses are plunging and straining in their harness.

"Be careful you two!" Ma cries. "O-h-h-h, this is just what I was afraid would happen!"

Ma and the girls continue to scream and I have a difficult time not joining them. I put my arm around Ma and try to comfort her.

"Pa will calm them, not to worry!" I shout. However, I'm not so sure myself. Uncle Ed still cannot get a hold on Andy's bridle and poor Toby is so excited he is rearing too. The cutter is rocking back and forth. Then Wild Andy suddenly leaps forward, dragging confused Toby with him!

The cutter speeds ahead and careens along the lane. I quickly look back to see what had happened to Pa and Uncle Ed. They are both running as fast as they can after the cutter. Of course, they are no-match for the horses who are now galloping at full speed. The fresh snow on the lane is not slowing them at all. Big clumps of snow are flying off their thundering hooves striking the front of the cutter.

Doc is sitting with his feet braced against the dashboard of the cutter and is pulling back hard on the reins. I can hear his high-pitched voice calling "Whoa Andy, whoa Toby!" repeatedly. The team does not slacken their pace.

I know up ahead is a rather deep ditch into which snow has drifted. It is full of snow and the team will not see it before they run into it. If the horses run into that deep snow at this speed they will stumble and fall, the cutter will crash into them and the horses and my family will all be terribly hurt. What can I do?

I quickly climb into the front seat with Doc, "What can I do?"

"Climb out onto the tongue, work your way forward and get hold of each bridle. Then pull the horses' heads together. Call Andy and Toby by name. You have to distract them."

I have seen Pa walk out onto the tongue of a wagon to calm a runaway team. Those circumstances were similar to now but Pa is a lot bigger and stronger than I am. He is not here! Now I have to do it! I know there are plenty of places on the harness to hang onto but the tongue of the cutter is jumping about as the horses lunge forward. The footing will be very difficult and hunks of snow flying from the hooves of the speeding horses will strike me.

After dropping my mittens on the seat, I climb over the dashboard. I will have a better grip on the harness with bare hands. I hear Ma screaming my name and the word "don't." At first, I hold onto the taunt reins then I get hold of the traces and slide my feet ahead on the tongue. If I fall, the cutter will run right over me and that will mean the end of me! If I'm not stepped on by a horse first that is.

I must help my family!

Only seconds are going by but it seems like forever before I get to Andy's head and hang onto his bridle with one hand and grab Toby's bridle with the other. As I speak calmly to them, I pull their heads together as hard as I can.

Their eyes are wild with fear and their breath is coming in great gasps. Clouds of steam pour from their wide-open nostrils.

At first, my efforts have no effect and fear wells up in me because I know we must be near the ditch now. My body is bouncing up and down with the movement of the tongue. My feet are sliding! I'm going to fall!

Doc yells, "Do it again as hard as you can! Give it all you have got!"

I give the bridles another tug and yell, "Whoa Andy, whoa Toby, calm down boys." This time it seems to work for their heads turn toward me and they begin to slow. Doc calls for them to whoa again and by pulling hard on the inside reins is able to pull their heads further toward the center. Their pace slackens more and they finally stop, gasping for breath, heads down, front legs spread, sides heaving, nostrils flared.

Pa and Uncle Ed run up in a few moments and take hold of the horse's bridles. Boy, am I glad to see them! I'm shaking all over. After carefully making my way back to the cutter, I climb in and immediately sit down. Carolyn is still crying and Ma is trying to comfort her. Ruthie and Mary are clutching each other but soon stop when they realize all is well. They begin to pat me on the back and head but I'm too tired to acknowledge them. My heart is beating a mile a minute. I'm exhausted but feel proud of my accomplishment.

Doc gives me a crushing hug. "You have done well to stop the team; it is just in time because the ditch is only a few yards ahead."

After seeing that the horses are too tired to run further, Pa comes back to the cutter, picks me up into his arms, and gives me an even bigger hug.

"You did a splendid job. I'm very proud of you. You accomplished a very difficult task."

I feel wonderful!

I climb into the back seat and am glad to sit with Ma and the girls. Pa and Uncle Ed slowly lead the horses through the ditch and along the lane until we reach the Ridge Road. They get into the cutter and let the team slowly make their way home. We had lost my sled during the confusion but I can find it after school tomorrow.

It is great to get home. Ruthie even helps me finish my part of the chores.

"Danny, you were wonderful with the horses this afternoon! You saved us all from dying!" she exclaims when she meets me in the horse barn.

It is unusual for me to be on the receiving end of anything positive from Ruthie so I'm pleasantly surprised.

"I don't know about dying but we could have had a bad wreck," I say.

"This is no time for you to be modest; you know you saved us all." Then she gives me a very wet kiss on the forehead.

"Yuck, what did you do that for? I don't need any big sister kisses." I wipe my forehead with my dirty hand.

"I'll bet you would like it if Rachel gave you a kiss. I'll tell her all about how you saved us when I see her in class tomorrow. Amelia and I see the way you look at her."

Amelia is one of Ruthie's school friends even though she is only in the sixth grade.

"Don't you dare tell her, don't even talk to her, especially about me. Please, please leave me out of your girl talk. Rachel doesn't even know I'm sitting behind her most of the time.

"Boy, I dread going to school tomorrow." This just sort of pops out of my mouth and I instantly regret saying anything about it.

Ruthie doesn't look surprised, "I know Billy is giving you a hard time, is there anything I can do? Do you want me to speak to Miss Spaulding for you?"

"No! Just stay out of it. I have enough problems at school without you adding to them. Don't say anything to anybody about me."

"Well, you needn't to be so harsh. I'm just trying to be helpful."

"Thanks for the offer but I don't need or want your help. Your meddling will just make things worse."

"All right, Danny, but I think you should find help from someone."

We finish cleaning the pigpen in silence and walk to the kitchen.

Ma heats some beef soup she had made the day before and we have that for supper along with bread and butter, then it is off to bed.

It is very cold in my room because the wind is again hitting on that side of the house. Ma has given me a hot brick, which I place under the covers about where my feet will be. I undress quickly, pull on my flannel nightshirt, and crawl under the covers. My room is much too cold for reading so I put out my candle, draw the wool blankets, and flannel sheet up over my head. Soon I'm nice and toasty.

Sleep will not come. I keep thinking about the runaway team and how close we all came to disaster. If Doc had not been there, I would not have known what to do.

Suddenly I become aware of a noise outside one of my windows. It is a scratching noise. I have not heard a noise like it before. It makes me feel somewhat sick to my stomach. What can it be? I want to get up and look but I don't dare! Crawling deeper into my bed doesn't help. The eerie sound is still there.

Finally, I ask myself, this is silly, what is there to be afraid of? Here I'm inside the house and on the second floor. What can possibly be there that could hurt me? I jump out of bed onto the very cold floor and instantly wish I had stayed under the covers. Wow! It is cold.

I look out the window and can see nothing. After scraping the frost off the glass, I still can't see anything that could make that kind of noise.

It occurs to me that something is hitting the side of the house, not the glass. I look down and to the right and I can see that it is just a tiny tip of a limb from the walnut tree that stands near the corner of the house. The wind is just right to affect it that way. All that fear for nothing. I feel very stupid and am glad I did not awaken anyone in the house about it. I'm very glad I settled the problem for myself.

I look out the window again to admire the moonlight on the new snow. It is all sparkles and beautiful and almost bright as day. I know that if I press my right cheek on the glass and if I try hard, I can see the corner of the horse barn.

There is something moving just where the pig yard begins. I can't believe my eyes. I look again. It is still there and it is something quite big but only slightly darker in color than the shadow of the barn. I wonder to myself, what would be out on a cold night like this? I look harder and then see it more clearly. It is the cougar! The cougar is going to get into the pig yard. The pigs are safe for the night as they are in the barn basement. What if the cougar comes during the day.

Sure enough, the big cat is looking to get himself a pig. Perhaps he felt it would be easier than catching a deer.

This was just what Pa, Doc and Uncle Ed had been talking about, and afraid might happen. Where is Buster? I wonder. It is one of his jobs to let us know if something is wrong in the yard.

I pull on my pants and a heavy shirt and quietly open my bedroom door. There is Buster. Someone had let him in the house for the night. Guess one of the girls felt it was too cold for him in the woodshed. No wonder he didn't know about the intruder over by the pig yard.

He looks up at me with his sleepy black eyes. He has a guilty look on his face for he knows he isn't supposed to be there. Buster follows me down the back stairs to the kitchen and woodshed.

"Buster, there is a cougar in the pig yard. Get out there and chase him away," I say aloud. "Be sure to stay away from him so he can't get hold of you though."

Back in my room, I quickly look out my window. Sure enough, I can see dutiful Buster running about near the pig yard but can see no cougar. It is gone.

There is no need to tell anyone what I had seen now because all is safe. I will tell them in the morning. I jump back into bed, and gratefully pull the covers over my head. I put my feet on the warm brick and soon get comfortable. This time I fall directly to sleep.

CHAPTER 6

▼

SCHOOL

"Danny, get up and go do your chores," Ruthie yells.

I moan and roll over, guess the hero worship from yesterday is gone. After sliding out of bed, I put on my work clothes and run down the back stairs to the kitchen. Only Ma is there, getting breakfast ready for us children. The men have already eaten.

"Morning, Ma, how are you?"

"I'm well, how is yourself?" she replies while stirring the oatmeal. "Did you sleep well, were you warm enough?"

"Oh, I'm fine and was nice and warm. Couldn't get to sleep though and looked out my window and saw the cougar over by the pig yard." I don't say anything about Buster failing to be on the job. The girls would be in trouble for letting him in the house.

"You did!" Ma exclaims. "Be sure and tell the men when you see them. I will talk to your Pa about it also. It looks like the cat will have to be taken care of soon as it is getting rather bold."

"Do you think Pa will shoot it?"

"I expect so. We can't have it wandering around as if it owns the place. Now get a move on so you can eat a good breakfast before going to school.

Doc is going to drive you children because it is still very cold. Bundle up well before you go out to do your chores."

"But Ma, if we keep the stock locked up the cat can't hurt anything."

"True for now, what are we going to do in the spring when the animals have to be let out?"

"I don't know, Pa and Doc will think of something."

"Stop worrying about the cat, it has to be dealt with, and that is that."

"But Ma, it has the right to live its life, doesn't it?"

Ma replies with her usual common sense, "Yes, it does have the right to live. However, it is a vicious killer. You know it must eat too. We would have to live in constant worry about it killing our livestock. Worse yet, it could attack one of us. Now you know all this. Put the cougar out of your mind and do the things you are supposed to do. I don't want to hear any more concern over the cat."

"Yes'm," I say, looking at the floor. I pull on my heavy clothes. Ma had brought my boots into the kitchen so they will be warm.

"Thanks for warming my boots, Ma," I yell as I run out the kitchen door. Once out of the woodshed I realize just how cold it is and that it is still quite windy. Boy, am I glad we are getting a ride to school.

I run quick as I can to the corner of the barn where I had seen the big cat. Buster follows me, bounding along side, but doesn't seem the least bit interested. I can find no tracks for the blowing snow has covered whatever marks had been there.

I set to work doing my chores.

"You pigs are lucky you have a nice safe place in which to live," I speak as if they can understand me. "There was a big cat out here last night looking to have you for a midnight snack." They don't look at all concerned; guess they know we will look out for them.

I scramble up the stairs to get water and find ice in the watering trough. It is thin so I have no trouble getting what is necessary for the pigs. Then it is time to pitch some hay for the horses, give them their oats, and fill their water pails. I give Jim and Dan an extra measure of oats as they are going to haul logs today.

I hurry back to the house for I know by this time breakfast will be waiting for me.

Ruthie has beaten me once again, and is already dressed in her school outfit and has most of her breakfast eaten.

"Good morning everyone, the cougar came for a visit last night," I announce while I wash up.

"How do you know, smarty pants?" Ruthie smirks.

"I saw it out my window that is how I know."

Mary gasps and asks, "It didn't get any of the pigs did it?"

For some reason, the pigs are her favorites.

"No, of course not, they are all locked in the barn. You know that, don't be silly," I reply sharply.

"Danny, be nice to your little sister, that is no way to talk to her," Ma scolds. "She was just showing her concern."

"Yes Ma, you are right," I answer. "Sorry I spoke to you that way, Mary."

"That's all right, Danny, I know you didn't mean to be mean." Mary says, blinking away the tears that form so quickly in her blue eyes.

I know I have hurt her feelings though and will try to do something nice for her on the way to school for I don't want her to feel bad. After changing into my school clothes, I eat my breakfast of hot oatmeal, bread, grape jam, and milk. My books and slate are in their heavy cloth bag. When I come back to the kitchen Doc is waiting and the girls are dressed for outdoors.

Ma is telling Doc about my seeing the big cat during the night. "Charles must do something about that cougar. Danny saw it by the pig yard last night."

"That so, Misses? It sure is a shame it will have to be killed. Charles had better act soon before that big cat attacks one of us or Buster."

I'm trying not to think about the poor cougar. "Mary, you can give me your book and I will carry it in my bag," I suggest. "Then you will be able to keep your hands in your pockets to keep them warm."

She looks down at me and I know I have made things right between us. I can see Ma smiling approvingly at me behind Mary's back.

"Oh, thanks Danny."

"Come on you two, Doc is awaiting and so is school," Ruthie exclaims in her bossy way.

"Why do you only seem to speak to Mary and me when you want to tell us what to do?" I ask.

"Because you two need a push to get you going. Both of you spend far too much time daydreaming," sneers our big sister.

"Children, children, get a move on! Doc is waiting. He will pick you up at the school at four o'clock if the weather is still bad." Ma continues with, "Danny, you may walk to Uncle Jerome's after school if you wish. Pa and Uncle Ed will be delivering a load of wood there this afternoon."

"Doc will find your sled after he drops you off at school this morning." She gives each of us a hug, a kiss and a "Stay warm and work hard in school."

"All right Ma," I say, glad that I can go to Uncle Jerome's place. I'm also relieved that Doc will look for my sled. It was last year's Christmas present and my Pa had made it for me. I couldn't bear to think of losing it or to have it broken.

When we walk to school, we usually take a short cut by the vineyard and through some woods and do not take the road that goes from the ridge down toward the lake. Our footpath takes about half a mile off our over two-mile walk. This path is not useable now that we have so much snow. It would be much too difficult for us to walk. When the men get to it, they will pack down a path for us by using a horse to drag a length of log along the trail.

Into the small, one-horse cutter we climb, Doc and the two girls and I all scrunched together on the single seat. Doc has hitched Kit to the sleigh. It is a little strange, almost funny to see the huge workhorse harnessed to the little cutter.

The grays will rest today after their exertions of yesterday.

We wrap ourselves well in the horse blanket and Ma gives us two hot bricks for our feet.

Off we go, the bells on Kit's harness are making beautiful music. Doc urges the big horse into a rumbling trot and we make good time. My face is becoming cold so I pull my scarf up over my nose and chin as the girls had done. Ah, that is much better.

I dread going to school. I like our school and our teacher, Miss Spaulding. Billy Marshall picking on me is what I don't like.

We thud up to our one room school building. "Thanks for the ride," we say.

"Thanks for looking up my sled, Doc. I hope it wasn't damaged yesterday."

"I'm sure I will find it all right, Danny," Doc says.

Ruthie says, "We will see you about four o'clock."

"Bye, bye," Mary calls. "Have a nice day."

"Have a good day," Doc says. "And work hard in school." He turns Kit around in the schoolyard and starts back.

The three of us walk into the cloakroom of the school and begin taking off our many outer garments. We hang them on our assigned hooks and place our boots neatly beneath them.

Our lunch pails go on a shelf along with our hats and mittens. Today we bring a meal of thick slices of bread and butter, cookies, and apples. Sometimes we also have a piece of cheese, sausage, or meat. Ma always gives us a quart container of milk, which Ruthie divides among us. We carry all this food in two tin dinner pails, one for our lunch, and one for the milk. Our tin cups hang by their handles on a leather strap around the milk can.

By this time, the door to the schoolroom opens and Bully Billy walks into the cloakroom. Teacher assigned him the task of ringing the school bell but he seems to forget all about it when he sees me. A knot of worry forms in my stomach.

"Hello, Danny, you're here. I thought that perhaps you would not make it to school today. I see you have your caretaker with you," as he often calls Ruthie.

"Hello, Billy, we made it to school all right. We got a ride. Glad you are here. Did you have to walk?" I ask with some concern.

"Oh, got a ride, did you. What's the matter, too weak to walk?" Billy speaks in his usual bitter tone of voice.

"We have further to go than you do and Mary is much too little to walk that far in this weather," I explain.

"Oh, sure, blame your ride on your little sister who is taller than you. I'll bet it was as much for you as it was for her," Billy sneers.

"The ride was for all three of us, Billy, and will you please get out of the way, I for one want to go into the classroom where it is warm," Ruthie says. "You had better ring the bell before Miss Spaulding comes out here to do it herself," she continues in her best bossy tone.

"Butt out caretaker, and stop meddling I'm talking to your very little brother," Billy taunts as he begins to pull on the rope that rings the schoolhouse bell. He had already put up the flag on the outside flagpole. These are the jobs, along with keeping the fire going, and bringing in water, of the oldest boy in the school.

It really isn't necessary to ring the bell today. Any child coming to school will not be stopping to play along the way and will not need any reminding of the time. It is just too cold.

Ruthie gives Mary and me a shove toward the door and we all file into the classroom. We sit in our seats after warming ourselves at the wood stove. How good the heat feels on a very cold day like this!

The room organization is by age of student, the youngest up front, and the oldest in the back.

The classes only go to grade eight. If you want to continue your studies after that, you have to go into town for high school. Because of the distance, these advanced students board with someone during the week and only come back to their farm home for the weekends.

Ruthie is not looking forward to having to do this next year but she enjoys school and that is the only way to continue. She likes to pretend she likes the idea of living in town but I think she is just covering up her true feelings.

Many students never even get through the eighth grade because their labor is needed at home. Billy only comes to school during the harshest part of the winter because his Pa needs him to work on the farm.

He would be a good student if he could come to class more. He excels in arithmetic and often helps some of the lower grade students who needed it. Ruthie and I feel a little sorry for him—when he is not picking on me that is. It is lucky for me he can't come to school every day.

Bully Billy bumped into me while we were on the schoolhouse steps the other day. This caused me to crash into Stan and knock him down.

"Hey!" Stan yells.

"I'm sorry I hit you, Stan," I say as I help him to his feet. "Billy bumped into me. You're not hurt, are you?"

"Nah, I saw him. I think he did it on purpose."

"You may be right."

"Why is he giving you so much trouble?" Stan asks.

"I don't know but I am sure going to find out!"

There are twenty-one children in the school when all are present. Not all classes have a student and some have several.

Cousin Jay goes to school in School District Number Five that is closer to his house while Cousin Ada is already going into town during the week to attend high school. Ruthie will be staying in the same boarding house with her when she starts ninth grade next September. This makes the thought of the big change to high school a little easier to take for Ruthie but not for me. I will miss my big sister—bossing and all.

Billy's desk is next to Ruthie's because they are the only eighth grade students. Billy is a year older than Ruthie is. He did not finish all his eighth-grade work last year because of missing so much school. He has to come to school an extra year to make up the work so he will have his eighth grade certificate. Miss Spaulding is helping him with this.

Billy's father said he didn't want him to waste any more time in school but the teacher and the head of the School Board convinced Mr. Marshall of its importance.

The schoolroom front wall has pictures of the United States Presidents on it. They start with George Washington in the left corner and ending with the current President, Grover Cleveland. There is a small U. S. flag near President Washington's picture. Framed copies of the Deceleration of Independence and Preamble to the Constitution also hang on this wall.

The right side wall has blackboards on it. The left sidewall is mostly tall windows to let in whatever light is available. There is a big clock on the back wall where the students cannot see it without turning around in their seats. But we can hear it ticking.

There are several students in Mary's second grade class and three in my fourth grade class, Rachel, and my best friend, Stan. Stan's full name is Stanley but no one had better call him that to his face, except the teacher and of course, his parents. Stan is usually good natured, perhaps that is why I like him so much. His father is Mr. Hicks who presents the Sunday school lesson.

Billy finishes ringing the school bell and sits at his desk just as Miss Spaulding calls the children to attention by ringing a little hand bell she keeps on her desk.

"All right children, settle down now, please. Good morning, I'm very glad to see that so many of you made it to school today in spite of the weather."

Miss Spaulding lives with one of the families that have one or more students in the school. Ruthie, Mary, and I know that it will be our family's turn next to board the schoolteacher. I'm not looking forward to that. Miss Spaulding is nice but I have enough schooling at school.

Teacher is a young woman, rather tall and slender and quite good looking in a plain sort of way. She wears her golden-yellow curly hair piled on top of her head as many of the town women do. Some strands of hair escape from the hairpins and she often has to push them away from her face. The unruliness of teacher's hair fascinates me as all of our family has straight hair.

Generally, the students like her and enjoy having her as their teacher. This is her third year at our school, which is in School District Number Twenty.

"Stanley, I believe it is your turn to lead the class in the Pledge of Allegiance to the Flag."

Poor Stan groans quietly because he hates to get up in front of the class. I give him a little poke with my elbow by way of encouragement and smile at him as he stands.

Just then, I'm hit in the back of the head by a dry bean. I try to ignore this as I stand. Miss Spaulding evidently did not see it. There is little doubt where it came from.

"I pledge allegiance to the flag of the United States of America, and to the Republic for which it stands, one nation, indivisible, with freedom and justice for all," we recite with teacher.

Another dry bean hits me, this time on the shoulder. As Stan sits with an obvious look of relief on his face, I turn to look Billy's way. Billy is grinning at me and chuckling.

"Danny, eyes front please, we are about to start class," teacher says.

"Yes'm. I'm sorry." I feel my face is hot and I know red with embarrassment. I immediately sit at attention with my hands clasped on top of my desk. I can feel my big sister's disapproving look from behind me. Billy has gotten me into trouble again.

"Ruth, will you please help grades two and three with their reading and spelling?" This is fine with Ruthie because she wants to teach someday. "Seventh and eighth graders, read your geography lesson and I will be there to help you shortly. Fourth, fifth, and sixth graders check your arithmetic homework and we will start a new lesson."

And so it goes through the day, Miss Spaulding working with one group of students and then another until all of us have been helped.

We work our arithmetic problems on a slate, each taking a turn or sometimes on the blackboard. We have a small globe to look at and a thin little book for geography. Each class level has their own reading and spelling books. A slate is used for practice but there aren't enough of these for everyone if all the children are in the school that day.

There aren't enough writing books to go around so we have to take turns with them too. We practice our writing in a bound student's book using pen and ink. These are carried on from one year to the next because paper is precious and not to be wasted.

The day goes by rather quickly, the older children helping the younger or slower ones and the teacher helping us all.

Several times each day, when he has the chance, Billy does something mean to me. He trips me when I am returning to my seat after getting a drink from the water pail. He also sometimes made a loud noise while I am reciting my lessons, disrupting the whole class. Billy even drops several dead flies in my inkwell, puts snow in my boots in the cloakroom, and pelts me with snowballs when we boys go outside for lunch recess on one of the warmer days.

The snowball combat isn't too bad because I'm quite good at packing and throwing them. I have to be good at something. I hit Billy several times but this resulted in Billy pushing snow down inside the back of my coat. Then I have all the afternoon with a cold wet shirt.

The worst thing is the time Billy managed to lock me in the boy's privy! He somehow stuck a stick in the latch so it would not open. One of the other boys heard me calling for help and let me out.

This was the last straw. I long to retaliate and play some mean trick on Billy or get some of my friends together and gang up on him in some way. I know it is wrong. Do unto others as you would have them do unto you really applies in Billy's case.

"Billy, why are you picking on me?" I ask while we are playing in the schoolyard. I do not want to involve the teacher or Ruthie because I want to resolve this problem myself.

"What do you mean?" Billy asks. He has his usual smirk on his face.

"You know what I mean all right," I say sharply. "You keep playing dirty little tricks on me to cause trouble. The days you put snow in my boots I have to walk all the way home with wet feet. Please tell me why you are picking on me. You don't pick on any of the other boys, just me."

My cheeks burn with anger when a silly grin slides across Billy's face. I try to take no notice. I long to escape the encounters with Billy that lay ahead but I have no idea how. I know I have to establish the why before I can figure out the how.

"How come you are picking on me?" I ask once again. This time Billy's face is unsmiling.

"I don't like you that's why," Billy spits out.

"But why don't you like me?"

"That is none of your business, little boy."

"Come on, Billy. You must have a reason."

"All right squirt. You irritate me because you get to come to school every day and I can't, that's why," Billy growls. "Your Pa wants you to come to school. Mine doesn't. I can only come a few weeks out of the year and have no chance of being able to go to high school. Even if there is enough money to let me go to town to school, my Pa will not let me because he wants me to do farm work."

"I long to live and work in town as a shopkeeper or as a bookkeeper. I love to do arithmetic and am good at it. My Pa needs me to do farm work because he can't afford a hired hand as your Pa can. Your Pa has two men to help him and I'm the only one my Pa has. My brothers are too young to be of any help."

"You are going to receive your eighth grade certificate this year aren't you Billy?"

"Yes, but only because Miss Spaulding has taken pity on me and is giving me so much extra of her time. I still won't be able to go to high school next year."

"Well, at least now I understand why you are picking on me. I don't see how it is helping you any though."

"It makes me feel better to give you a hard time because you usually have things pretty easy. Do you understand now?"

"Yes, I guess so," I mummer. "But what am I going to do about it?"

"There is nothing you can do about it, just take it," Billy grins. "I like to see the look of anxiety on your face."

"Isn't there something I can do to help you get to go to high school?"

"What can a little runt like you do to help me?" Billy growls.

We are called in from recess and the discussion with Billy ends.

Miss Spaulding has noticed there are hard feelings shown by Billy toward me. "Danny," she said one day while we were alone in the cloakroom, "What is going on between you and Billy?"

"Oh, nothing special," I say trying to put a smile on my face.

"It looks to me like he is picking on you. You aren't doing anything to cause this trouble are you?"

"No, teacher, he just doesn't like me, I guess."

"Nonsense, there has to be some cause. I can't help you if you won't help yourself."

"Thank you, Miss Spaulding," I say as I head out the door. "I will take care of the problem myself, somehow."

CHAPTER 7

▼

UNCLE JEROME

At four o'clock, Doc picks up the girls from school. He is driving the small cutter but this time has Bess hitched to it.

"Danny, I found your sled all right. It was near where the horses had spooked. Your knot came untied. You had better practice tying knots. Sometime it might be very important skill for you. The sled is not damaged."

"Thanks very much, Doc. Will you please help me with my bowline? Must be I didn't tie it correctly. I need to know how to tie many more knots."

I'm glad my sled is all right because it means a lot to me to have the sled to ride down hill with and after all, Pa had made it just for me. It is a good sled too.

"Sure, Danny, we can work on it right after supper." Doc clucks to Bess, and he and the girls head for home.

The afternoon is still miserably cold and windy but I want to visit with Uncle Jerome and Aunt Liz. Uncle Jerome's last name is also Lee and he is my great-uncle. Aunt Liz's full name is Elizabeth Bailey Lee. She is my great-aunt and they are my Pa's Uncle and Aunt. It is only another two miles down the road to their little house, which is situated on the shore of the east branch of the lake.

Uncle Jerome earns his living mostly by hunting, trapping, and fishing, keeps a few chickens, a cow and a horse, and has a vegetable garden. Pa and Ma help them now and then when needed.

During the second year of the War of the Rebellion Uncle Jerome and two of his brothers enlisted in the Union Army at Troy, New York. One of the Baker boys, Alderman Baker, joined with them. The Baker family is linked to the Lee family by marriage.

Uncle Jerome became a member of an ordnance company as a teamster. He drove a six-mule hitch, which pulled a canvas-covered wagon that usually carried ammunition! His duty, along with driving the team, was to take care of his mules and wagon.

Uncle often was involved, along with his company, in great difficulties of one sort or another. One of the worst was when they had to drive their heavily loaded wagons through deep, thick mud, which could be up to the bellies of the mules. At such times, the teamsters would unhitch from one wagon and combine the mules so there would be an eight-mule hitch to move one wagon!

Mules, wagon and teamsters would be covered in mud and soaking wet when it rained.

It was often difficult to find enough food and water for the team and himself when they were on the road. Sometimes, even when in a bivouac, there was not enough to eat. At least he had a dry place to sleep, on top of the ammunition when the wagon was loaded or in it when it was empty. Uncle Jerome felt sorry for the men who had to sleep on the ground.

I walk down the hill, bundled up against the cold. The effort of walking with all my winter clothes on is keeping me warm.

In front of me is Keuka Lake, dark gray-blue, reflecting the darkness of the sky. The lake has not frozen here in spite of the cold weather. White caps are common and darker patches of water mark the gusts of stronger wind. The white caps make a dramatic contrast with the dark water. Big waves are crashing onto the shore on the other side of the lake. I never get tired of looking at the water. It is a thing alive and is always changing.

I can see the lumber bobsled in the yard as I walk down the lane to the house. The sled is empty. Must be the firewood has been stacked and the horses are in the barn, I think to myself. I won't have much to do as Pa and Uncle Ed have the wood unloaded and stacked in the woodshed already. I walk up on the back porch glad to be at my destination.

Pa opens the door for he had watched me making my way toward the house and I step into the warm and cozy kitchen. It is a small room that seems to be filled with the cookstove, work shelf, table, and chairs. All are sitting around the kitchen table, enjoying coffee and some johnnycake Aunt Liz had baked.

"Hello everyone, mighty cold day out there," I remark as I shut the door.

"Come and sit here at the table by the stove and warm up," Aunt Liz says in her quiet voice. "Have some johnnycake and I will warm some milk for you."

Her soft brown eyes and gentle ways make me feel welcome whenever I come to her house. Her very long white hair, twisted into a braid, is wound tightly around her head. She is a tiny woman.

"Thanks, Aunt Liz. Johnnycake is always good," I say as I pour molasses over the warm cake. You must have gotten the wood unloaded and stacked early, Pa"

"Yes, we just finished and are warming ourselves," Pa says. "How was school today, were there many children absent?"

"Almost everyone came," I reply. "Miss Spaulding was pleased. Doc came and picked up the girls. He had found my undamaged sled. How are you Aunt and Uncle?"

"Not bad for old folk," Uncle Jerome replies. He always says this when anyone asked him how he and Aunt Liz are.

"Do you have any chores for me to do?" I ask.

"Nope, your Pa and Ed have got us all caught up and much obliged we are to them."

"Do you have any stories of the war?" I ask.

"I knew you were going to ask that," Uncle Jerome laughs with a twinkle in his very light blue eyes.

He is a short man, thin and wiry with white long hair and a full white beard. He uses little silver-rimmed eyeglasses. Uncle too speaks softly but you know right away when he is being serious about his subject. This is how he is when he talks about his war experiences.

Uncle Jerome starts out by asking, "Did I ever tell you about what happened to me and my company at Gettysburg in Pennsylvania?"

He had told this tale before but I can never get enough of the story so I say, "Yes, but tell us again, please."

"Well," he starts, "It was early in July of '63 and very hot and dry. We all were suffering from thirst as we made trip after trip to the railroad, northeast of the town, to pick up ammunition for General Mead's Army of the Potomac."

"This battle around the town of Gettysburg had been going on for quite sometime already and it seemed we were making endless trips, night and day. There had been little time to eat or sleep and all of us, mules included, were dog tired and plum worn out."

"Our efforts were still needed though because there was sure to be more battle the next day, which was the third of July. We continued the best we could having no other orders."

"My company was making a delivery of artillery shells at Cemetery Hill and was just northeast of the ridge and therefore protected from the battle that was going on to the south and west. The racket was infernal."

"Then, suddenly, the shells from the Reb's cannon began to land among us! The crash of exploding shells was indescribable! Tremendous clouds of black smoke were everywhere! The Reb's were over shooting their mark along the ridge and their shells were falling on the reverse slope where we, the noncombatants were located."

"Our poor mules were just about mad with fear as were many of the men. Loud wails, moans, and screams could be heard from all directions. When an exploding shell hit one of the loaded ammunition wagons, the wagon just disappeared in a cloud of flame and black smoke!"

"Some of us ran and jumped into a shallow ditch hoping it would protect us, which it mostly did. I felt sick, weak, and ashamed that I was so frightened. Some of us started to get up when a shell exploded so close it knocked us all flat. After giving some comfort to a man who had a big gash in his arm, I looked at myself everywhere and only found a few holes and tears in my uniform. I was shaking all over."

"My mules ran off with my wagon and after the cannon fire stopped I went off to look for them and pick up the pieces if I could. I never did see them again but heard word later they where were found miles away with no wagon left. It had been totally wrecked. The gunfire had only lasted a few minutes but it sure caused a lot of damage. I went to the company headquarters and got my new orders."

"Lee, find a loaded ambulance without a driver and take it to the rail station," my corporal told me.

"I was glad to have something useful to do and was also glad to get away from the battle area because the fighting was still going on. The almost constant moaning coming from the wagons kept me in continuous fear and concern."

"I made many trips, day and night, with my ambulance to the railroad and helped load the wounded on to the trains. Some of them were my teamster friends, many of whom died. Some of my friends were never to be seen again, blown to bits! The destruction was awful!"

"I can't understand why or how I escaped without a scratch. It was just the chance of war or someone looking out for me."

Tears are welling up in his expressive eyes and streaming down his wrinkled face, he blows his nose. Before long, all of us have to blow our noses.

By the way he described it, it was not hard to understand how the experience had moved him and changed him for life. Aunt Liz pats him on the shoulder, trying to console him. I wish I had not asked him about the battle that we now call the Battle of Gettysburg.

Suddenly Pa speaks, "Look how it is snowing. We had better be on our way."

The sky had grown quite a bit darker and small but many flakes are falling. Uncle Ed stands and starts to put on his outer clothes.

Aunt Liz says, "Thanks for the visit, Danny, and thanks for the fire-wood Charles and Ed. Give our best to everyone at your house and Henry's folks."

Uncle Ed nods in reply and says, "Come on Danny, you and I will get the team hitched."

"All right," I say as I start to struggle into my things. "Bye Uncle Jerome, bye Aunt Liz. Thanks for the johnnycake and milk."

"I'll be right there, just want to talk to Uncle for a minute," Pa states.

I know he is going to remind Uncle Jerome to ask for any help they might need during the winter and that he is going to send down some deer meat and other supplies in a few days.

Uncle Ed and I have Big Jim and Big Dan hitched to the bobsled in a few minutes. I'm not much help because I cannot reach most of the harness. I set my teeth in anger feeling once again that I'm next to useless to my family. Oh, why am I so short? My hands get cold quickly because I have them out of my mittens and soon I'm shivering.

Pa comes outside and takes the reins. Uncle Ed and I sit on the edge of the bobsled, each wrapped in a horse blanket, and soon I'm warm again. Pa is standing behind the team so he can see over their backs and view the road ahead.

He flicks the reins on their broad backs and calls, "Giddyap Jim and Dan." With a jingle and a jangle, we are on our way. I see Uncle and Aunt looking out their kitchen window as we drive down the lane and wave good-bye.

Snow is settling quickly but the team does not have any difficulties. They just keep plodding along up the hill as though nothing can stop them. I try to look across the lake. It is snowing hard, and it is very dark; I can't see anything of the other shore. The white caps are even more spectacular than before because the water is darker, dark as the sky.

Presently it is completely dark and Pa can no longer see the road. Uncle Ed gets off the sled and walks ahead of the team with a lantern. He had lit the lantern before we left the shelter of Uncle Jerome's barn. Slowly we make our way home. Uncle Ed gets back on the bobsled when we reach the ridge because the road is nearly clear of snow and is just icy in spots. We have no problem seeing the way.

It is a welcome sight to see the oil lamp in the front parlor window as we come toward our house. Its yellow glow cheerfully shows our way.

Buster is there in the yard to greet us with his usual joyful yelps and back flips. He quickly runs and jumps onto the sled.

"Hey, Buster! Were you waiting for us?"

"Woof, woof, woof," he barks.

"Good dog. You were waiting by the road for us in spite of the cold. Good dog!" Buster is beside himself with happiness. He is wagging his tail so fast it looks like it wants to fly right off.

After putting the bobsled in the shed, we begin to do our usual chores. I'm very hungry, as usual, but the chores have to be done before we can eat supper.

Ruthie and I have switched and it is now my turn to take care of the chickens and turkeys. We have a flock of Plymouth Rock chickens and Bronze turkeys. I go to the house to get some hot water for the chicken's mush. Ma meets me at the kitchen door with a kettle and I make my way to the poultry house, attached to the south side of the equipment shed. The front right corner of the equipment shed contains large bins of grain and mash.

After measuring the mash into a pail, I add the hot water and stir it to make a thick mush. After picking up a pail of buckwheat and dry corn, I make my way into the poultry house.

A loud series of clucks, squawks, and whirring of flapping wings greet me as I enter. There is nothing happier than a bunch of chickens and turkeys that are about to be fed. I pour the mush into several shallow pans and scatter the grain on the floor.

It is a necessity that I'm ready to defend myself from the rooster. He is a mean one all right and often flies up into my face in an attempt to peck my eyes. I have named him Mean Bill.

I hold my hands out ready to ward him off but for some unexplained reason he does not attack tonight. Perhaps he wants to eat too much because his supper is somewhat late.

My favorite hen, Helen, comes over to me. She half runs and half flies across the hen house. She eats her scrap of bread Ma had given to me just for her. Helen is my pet chicken. She hatched out in the fall and is starting to lay eggs. I hope she will be extra productive. Then she will be kept for egg production and not sold or put in the stew pot.

After mucking out the manure, replacing the straw, and filling their water pails, I check for eggs under any of the setting hens. Eggs are rare this time of year because the days are short and tend to be dark. Chickens need light and warmth to be encouraged to produce eggs. That is why there are so many windows in a chicken coop. I find only twelve eggs from our thirty or so chickens. This is not very good but is common this time of year.

CHAPTER 8

▼

BESS, ALMOST MY HORSE

Next Saturday morning, while we all are sitting at the breakfast table, Pa announces exciting news to Ruthie and me.

"Ruthie and Danny, I'm going to let you ride Bess once and awhile if she is not going to be needed for work. You are responsible for her grooming and whatever extra care Doc or I decide she needs. Remember she is not to be galloped under any circumstance. Doc has rigged a ladder to help you climb aboard her and will make a ledge for you to stand on in her stall so you can groom her."

"It is no disgrace to fall off but you are not to come home without the horse either riding or walking. Is this clear to you both?"

"Yes sir!" we echo.

"Thanks Pa we will take good care of her," I say.

"Yes, thanks Pa, we will take good care of her," Ruthie adds with a voice that is unusually joyful.

Pa continues, "You may also use her with the small cutter. Come spring I will get you a riding pony if you show you can properly take care of Bess. She is all your responsibility."

"Oh boy, just think, Ruthie, we will be able to visit folks and explore and everything!"

"Don't get too excited, Danny, we will still have our chores to do and taking care of a horse has just been added to that," Ruthie reminds me.

"I will enjoy grooming her," I exclaim.

"You would," she adds with scorn.

Wow, I'm thrilled, a horse to ride and to take care of for me! It is wonderful even if it is a huge draft animal and only the promise of a real riding horse in the spring. For once, my big sister didn't learn something new or get an additional privilege or responsibility ahead of me.

"Eat your breakfast and we will go out to the barn and start your horse care lessons," Pa says. "It takes lots of time and work to properly care for a horse," he adds in his best informative voice, "but it is time well spent. You know some of this already but a refresher won't hurt. Then you can go for a little ride."

Ma continues to cook pancakes but they do not cook fast enough for me. She carefully watches for the edges to brown and the batter to form bubbles before she turns them on the hot griddle. Steam rises from them as they cook and when she puts a fresh bit of butter on the hot griddle it sizzles and dances about while it quickly melts. It smells so-o-o-o-o-o good! Ruthie and I eat as fast as we can and Ma lets us go when Pa finishes his breakfast.

"Be extra careful around that horse you two. Do you hear me?" Ma calls.

"Yes'm, we will," we reply.

It is a relatively warm and pleasant day for winter on the bluff. There is no wind and the sun is bright, it is a good day to be outside. We pull on our old clothes and to the horse barn we go. Doc and Uncle Ed are there, grooming the horses. We stand by Bess and Pa begins to go through the routine of horse care. During each procedure, Pa stops and lets Ruthie and I finish.

"A horse is groomed at least once a day. This not only makes the animal look nice and clean but also is a way of making sure there are no injuries or other problems. Grooming each day keeps the horse comfortable with having people around it. I bet a vigorous brushing and then a rub down with a soft cloth feels great."

"The pick is used to remove any ice or stones from the hooves. Hoof checking is done every time the horse is used. After you have ridden her, she is to be rubbed down again to get off any sweat or dirt. Is all this clear?"

"It is clear, Pa." Ruthie and I say.

Pa continues with, "You must be very careful that the horse does not accidently pin and crush you against the side of the box stall if she should shift her weight. The horse does not do this on purpose and it is your responsibility to keep out of the way. When you are removing or putting on the bridle or halter, stand to one side of the horse's head so that if she should bolt she won't crash into you."

These safety instructions we already knew as we have been told them several times. I didn't mind hearing them again.

Bess looks at us with some concern in her big dark eyes. Her ears rapidly move about when another person speaks. She soon seems to accept this change in her usual care and acts as though she enjoys all the attention.

Then Doc shows us the special harness he had made for us to use to climb to her back. Pa explains that a tall stump or wooden fence will do well too. The harness will also serve as something for us to hold onto while we are riding. Doc places a potato crate for us to stand on under the wall pegs where the harness is kept.

I'm becoming worried; will I be able to use the harness to get to her back? What if Ruthie can do it and I can't? The thought of this kind of failure makes me feel sick to my stomach!

"Who is first," Pa asks as he leads Bess out of the barn.

"I'm," I say, trying to show my confidence. My big sister gives me one of her 'I will succeed and you will fail looks.' I wish I had let her go first.

"This harness looks great, Doc. Thanks for making it for us."

Doc says, "I hope it works well for you. It shouldn't be too much effort for you to get aboard."

After stepping up to Bess' side, I lower the rope ladder. Starting with my left foot as instructed up I go. It is difficult but I make it. I shift my weight forward on Bess' back to make room for Ruthie and up she comes. She pulls the ladder up and ties it to the harness with a short piece of rope. We are ready for our ride.

I take up the reins and say, "Giddyap Bess," with my best in charge voice and off we go. "You are a good girl, Bess," I say as I direct her around the pigpen and past our garden.

Ruthie and I take turns directing the huge horse around the barnyard and even around the house. We see Ma and the two girls looking out the window at us and wave as we thud by. The men have left us to our fun. Bess seems to enjoy the ease of walking without a wagon or plow attached to her.

Ruthie says, "Let's put her through the big snow drift." We plow right through even though the snow is up to Bess' belly.

After a few minutes of walking, Ruthie says, "I'm going to make her trot, hang on." Ruthie makes a clicking sound and says, "Come on Bess, let's go faster." Bess willingly moves ahead at a thumping trot. It is difficult to stay put on her back at first but we learn how best to do it.

We move to the barn. "Whoa Bess," we both say. After sliding off, we lead the horse to the water trough. When she has her fill, we remove the harness, bridle, and put on her halter. We give Bess a rubdown and check her hooves.

"Boy, that was fun," I say happily.

"It was all right."

"What do you mean, just all right, it was great!" I exclaim.

"It is a little childish to just go riding around the house, don't you think?" Ruthie says, trying to sound grown up.

"Well, as soon as we can, we will ride down to the lake and visit Uncle Jerome and Aunt Liz. How does that sound?"

"That is a good idea, little brother. Let me know when you are going and perhaps I will go with you."

As we step into the parlor, Mary demands to know when we are going to take her for a ride on Bess. Using my best adult voice, I explain, "We have other things to do besides ride the horse around the house. I don't see how you are going to be able to climb up on her anyway; it is a little difficult for me." I tell her. "Besides, you are too weak to be able to hang on and will fall off."

It is easy to see she doesn't want to hear that kind of an answer as I watch her run off to find Ma.

"You are mean, Danny. Ma, Ma!" she yells, "Danny won't take me for a ride on Bess."

Ma is in the kitchen and I smile to myself as I hear her quietly explain to Mary that she is too young to ride Bess and that she will just have to be patient until she grows a little older and bigger.

"Oh pooh! I can't do anything!" Mary wails as she walks past me.

For dinner, we have fried pork chops, boiled potatoes swimming in butter and preserved green beans from our garden. After I help clean the kitchen, I bring in some wood for Ma and take out the ashes.

Ruthie asks, "Do you want to go skating on the pond?"

"Sure, let's go," I reply, glad to have someone to skate with even if it is my big sister. I have some schoolwork to do but it can wait until after dark.

"Ma is it all right if Danny and I go skating or do you have something you want us to do for you?" Ruthie asks.

"Go right ahead and skate, just bundle up well and don't stay out too long. When you get back, you can help me with some house cleaning because Henry's folks are coming to dinner tomorrow. Your Pa saw your Uncle Henry on the road this morning and invited them."

"Thanks Ma, we won't be out very long and then we will be glad to help you," Ruthie says.

"You might be glad to help Ma," I whisper to Ruthie, "but I would rather work with the animals in the barns."

"We all have to do some things that we don't want to do," Ruthie explains. "Besides, it won't hurt you to do a little house work. If you, Mary, and I all work together, it won't take that long," she says as she tugs on her second pair of heavy wool stockings.

CHAPTER 9

▼

ICE SKATING

We pick up our clamp-on ice skates from the woodshed. The ice pond is not very far from the house in one of the fields that we sometimes use for pasture and some years' plant crops. Most of the snow has blown off the path that leads to the pond but I get a shovel anyway.

The pond is fed by a spring in the northwest corner. We know that area will not be frozen because the water coming from the ground prevents it. If we don't want a very cold bath, it is important we stay many yards away from this area. Even though the ice around it might look safe, chances are it would not be strong enough to hold our weight. The water is not very deep but it would be very dangerous if one of us fell through.

Pa and the men cut big blocks of ice from our pond near the end of winter when the ice is at its thickest. The ice blocks are hauled to our ice-house for storage. The icehouse walls are very thick wood planks that are insulated by sawdust. There is even sawdust between the rafters in the ceiling.

The ice we use in warm weather to keep our food cold and prevent spoilage. Pa also hauls ice from the lake if it freezes thick enough. The ice blocks do not stick together because a layer of sawdust is placed between them.

Just then, Ma calls to us to say Mary wants to come to the ice pond with us and to wait for her. She doesn't have any skates but can slide around on the ice in her boots. We wait in the woodshed for what seems hours before she comes out.

While waiting Ruthie and I discuss Christmas and the gifts we are making.

"Do you have the bird house finished, Danny?"

"Yes it is done. It doesn't look the way I want but it is all right. I always feel I could do a better job."

"Doing woodworking takes time and practice. I'm sure Mary will like it. She loves birds and it will be very nice to have a wren family living near the house. Do you know where you will put it in the spring?"

"Pa says the maple tree next to the lane would be a good place. How are the dress and bonnet for Carolyn's doll coming? Have you finished the shawl for Ma?"

"They will be done on time. I'm almost finished."

"I have completed Carolyn's doll," I say. "It looks pretty good if I do say so myself. I can't wait to see the expression on her face when she sees it. Here comes Mary, hush!"

Mary looks more round than usual because of all the clothes she has on. She has on her red coat and her matching pixie hood. Her muffler is wrapped around her neck and over her chin. What she has beneath her coat, must be in several layers.

Off we three go, I in the lead to break or shovel a path through the snow if it is too deep for us to walk easily. Buster soon discovers we are outside and joins in the party. He greets us with a wagging tail and a joyful yip and is eager to join in our fun.

We clean the snow from a large log by the pond so we can sit to put on our skates. Ruthie and I take turns cleaning snow from a patch of ice so we can skate on the clear dark ice.

My big sister is a very good skater and she is helping me to learn how to do some of the tricks she knows. I'm not having much success and keep falling. This pleases Ruthie a good deal.

"I don't think you are even trying, little brother," Ruthie taunts. "Watch me and do just as I do. You always try to add something to the move that messes you up. You're clumsy too."

"Well, you go so fast I can't see what you are doing with your feet. Can't you slow down just a little bit?"

"If I slow down I won't be able to do the trick. You try harder. Watch again." Ruthie flies off in a perfect spiral leaving me to stare at empty space.

Mary seems to be having a good time pretending to be skating and laughing at me when I fall.

"Stop kicking snow onto the ice we have cleared!" I shout. She thinks it is big fun and continues to do it just to cause trouble.

"Mary, stop that. I just shoveled that snow off. Please stop messing up the ice," I yell at her.

"Do you want to stay here with us or don't you?" Ruthie asks sharply. She is bent over Mary and has her face close to hers.

Mary gets that look on her face that means she is about to cry and Ruthie continues with, "You cry now and I will send you home."

Mary goes to sit on the log and pout and before very long begins to complain about being cold. Ruthie leans over her but I can't hear what she is saying.

I skate over to the far side of the pond where the wind has blown most of the snow off the ice. I'm shocked to find fresh cougar tracks!

There are some small trees and scrub brush there that gave the cat some cover. The animal must have been looking for small game.

This big cat was really acting strange! Why wasn't it in the woods hunting deer? Pa had said the cat would prefer places where there was lots of cover; these tracks are in a mostly open field. I will have to tell Pa the cat had been around again even though it will surly spell its doom.

"Ruthie, come over here and look at this," I shout.

"O-o-o-o-h-h-h-h! It is the cougar again, isn't it?" she cries as she slides to a stop.

"Yes, now Pa will really have to shoot it. It has been near the house twice. It makes me sad but we will have to tell him."

Ruthie and I take off our skates and back to the house, we trudge. The skating was fun while it lasted but now it is housework until time to do chores before supper. UGH!

Sunday morning comes and we get ready for Sunday school as usual. Again, there is a long wait for the three girls. I don't understand how my big sister can be so fast at doing her chores and so slow at getting ready for Sunday school.

After the meeting is over, Uncle Henry, Aunt Mertie, Cousins Ada, Jay, Warren, and Aldy come for Sunday dinner.

Ma remained home from Sunday school to finish preparations for the meal. Some of the work, such as baking the pumpkin pies and baking the rolls, she did on Saturday.

It sure was hard not to get into those pies for Saturday supper. We also have baked ham with raisin sauce, mashed potatoes, and baked acorn squash from our garden. It is the last of the squash until next year. Ruthie made the raisin sauce and she and I peeled the potatoes.

Aunt Mertie brought the fixings for ice cream and after dinner, we all sit in the front parlor taking turns cranking the ice cream machine. There is nothing better than pumpkin pie with vanilla ice cream on top.

We use Grandma's special dishes from her china cabinet for dinner and for the pie and ice cream.

Warren, Carolyn, and Aldy have a wonderful time playing with Clara. They take turns pulling around some large buttons tied to a string. Clara attacks the buttons just as if it is a mouse. She has all of us laughing until we can laugh no more.

Jay and I have just enough time left for some ice-skating before dusk. After putting on our play clothes and warm outer garments off we go. I know Ruthie and Ada want to come too but they have to stay to help clean up the kitchen. Poor girls!

Buster is not waiting for us to come out and play. He is not in the woodshed, or in the back yard or in the barnyard. I don't even see any fresh tracks of his. It is not like him to be missing. I know he isn't in the house this time.

"Wonder where Buster is," I ask Jay. "It is unusual for him to not be here. I hope he is all right."

"Oh, he is out hunting a rabbit or something," Jay suggests.

"Usually he sticks around the house pretty close when we are having dinner hoping for a hand out."

"He will show up, he is just having a good time somewhere." Jay adds.

"Might be," I reply. "Let me show you the cougar tracks on the other side of the pond."

"That sounds great," Jay says.

We don't have to do any shoveling because it has not been windy to blow the old snow around and there was no new snow overnight. After putting on our skates, we make our way over to the far side of the pond where I had found the big cat's tracks the day before. I point them out to Jay and he is fascinated.

"Let's look around and see if we can tell where the cat went," he suggests. "It sure looks like a big one by the size of its feet!"

"We can walk in the snow with our skates on." I say.

Before long, we come across a reddish-brown stain in the snow.

"Wonder what that is," Jay exclaims.

"Don't know," I say, "but it looks like blood!"

The snow is all messed up and the cougar tracks are hard to see because they are mixed up with some other tracks. I soon realize there are tracks of a dog there too.

"Buster's tracks!" I exclaim to Jay. Some of the cat tracks cover the dog tracks so we know the cat was after the dog! Poor Buster! A big lump forms in my throat! "Gosh, Jay, do you think the cat got Buster?"

"Donno, it doesn't look good!"

We follow the trail moving as fast as we can with our skates still on our feet. Occasionally there are more spots of reddish-brown in the snow. This we now know is blood! Poor, poor Buster, this is the end of him! I want to say this to Jay but feel saying it aloud will make it so.

I begin to call the dog. "Here Buster, here Buster, where are you?"

There is no answer. There is no happy dog with a wagging tail.

Finally, we hear a little faint yelp and I call again. "Here Buster, here boy!" Two more yelps and a whimper and finally there is Buster crawling out from under a tangle of wild raspberry bushes.

He is not wagging his tail this time and comes limping over to me. I know he has been badly hurt by the cougar for it is a struggle for him to walk.

We examine him and find he has a long cut in his left side and his left foreleg has been cut too. The wounds look very bad to me. There is lots of dried blood on his fur. At least he is alive!

"How are we going to get him home?" Jay asks. "He can't walk there hurt like that."

"I don't know, let me think," I say as I pat my pal Buster and feel over his body to see if he is hurt elsewhere. Dried blood mats his beautiful white fur. Ice and snow cake his heavy coat. He feels cold. Buster lies in the snow half-heartedly wagging his tail. He whimpers and squeaks a little and looks very pitiful.

"I got it! Let's put him on my coat and between us we can carry him. What do you think?"

"Sounds good to me," Jay answers. "How are we going to pick him up without hurting him?"

"We can just roll him onto my coat, can't we?"

We put our plan to work and Buster seems to understand we are trying to help him and doesn't move once we get him situated. He just slowly wags the very tip of his tail. The dog is quite heavy and when we get back to the pond, we put the coat and Buster on the ice, and pull and push him along.

Buster keeps licking my face as I lean over to push him across the ice. I try not to cry but tears form anyway. My mouth is dry and I can hardly swallow.

Someone must have noticed from the house that we were not skating and we can see Pa rapidly walking up the path toward us once we cross the pond.

"What happened?" Pa asks. "Ruthie noticed you weren't skating."

"Looks like Buster was attacked by the cougar. It was in about the same place I saw tracks yesterday." I reply.

"Here, I will carry him and you boys can take off your skates. It is all right boy, good Buster, it's all right Buster," Pa says as he gently picks up the dog after wrapping him in my coat. "Let's get a move on, boys."

Pa starts out rapidly and Jay and I have to run to catch up.

Buster looks like he is asleep. I'm afraid he is dead. I check to see if he is still breathing. He is! Tears well into my eyes and I blink hard to prevent my Pa or Jay seeing them.

"Pa," I ask, "do you think Buster will be all right?"

"I don't know; let's let your Ma look at him. She is the doctor in the family. She is good at fixing injuries and such. She will fix him up if it is possible."

Pa walks toward the house using his long stride with Buster in his big arms and Jay and I trot along behind him.

Ma meets us at the woodshed door. "Bring the poor thing right into the kitchen and I'll see what can be done for him," she says.

"What happened to him?" Ruthie asks her voice quavering.

"Guess he was attacked by the cougar," Pa says.

Uncle Henry and his folks leave to go home after wishing Buster well. It is starting to get dark and although they don't have very far to go, Aunt Mertie would rather be home by nightfall.

Mary, and Carolyn are peeking around Ma's skirts and my two little sisters are already crying and whimpering. Ruthie is trying to put up a good front but I can see tears in her hazel eyes. I try not to look at my sisters for I know I will really begin to cry if I do.

"Is Buster going to die? Poor Buster!" Mary cries with a faltering voice. "Ma, will Buster die?"

Pa carefully puts Buster down in the center of the kitchen floor and I hang up my coat and hat and put my boots and skates in the woodshed. I put away Pa's outer garments too.

"Danny, go get your father's razor. This does not look to bad, Mary. If the dog will let me, I will have him cleaned up in no time. Ruthie, please go and get my little sewing scissors from my sewing box. Mary, please get a pan of warm water and the bar of soap off the wash table," Ma directs.

Ma cuts away the hair and dry blood around the wounds with the scissors, shaves the skin free of hair with Pa's straight razor, and washes the injured areas very gently with soap and water. She feels the dog's body to try to decide if he is hurt inside.

"Buster feels very cold. I think getting him warm again is the most important thing we can do for him. Was he here for breakfast, Danny?"

"No, I left some bread and meat in his dish this morning and it is still there."

"He has been hurt and laying in the cold for quite sometime, then," Ma says. "Mary, warm a little bit of milk for him and if he drinks it you can heat some more and break up some bread and melt some butter in it."

"Yes, Ma."

I sit on the kitchen floor, hold Buster's head in my lap, and try to comfort him and keep him quiet. He keeps licking my face and hands. Buster is making little whimpering sounds. He occasionally wags his tail a little and looks around at us sadly.

Pa gets Buster's bed from the woodshed and puts it near the stove so it can begin to warm.

"The wounds are not very deep so I think they will heal all right without sewing them closed. I'm not sure Buster would let me do it anyway," Ma explains. "He seems to have lost a lot of blood though."

We all sit on the kitchen floor to watch Ma clean Buster's wounds and to give him what comfort we can. It reminds me of the times Ma had cleaned our skinned knees and elbows with loving care and kissed away our tears.

Ma turns to me and says, "You can keep him in the kitchen until he is better. Get the old quilt to make a bed with and your pillow and blanket. You can sleep here with him tonight and keep him quiet so the wounds will heal."

"Thanks, Ma. Do you think he will be all right?" I ask.

"Yes, if the wounds stay clean, he should be his old self in no time," she says with a bright smile.

"Oh Ellen, you have done it again. I thought he was a goner for sure," Pa exclaims.

Pa carefully places the dog in his bed near the warm stove. He seems a little better already. Buster drinks the warm milk that Mary fixed for him and she makes a second dish. He eats that too.

"Danny, I want to talk to you in the parlor," Pa says loudly.

"Yes, sir." I meekly follow him knowing I'm going to get a talking to. Maybe even punished.

"Son, what were you thinking when you and Jay followed the cougar tracks? I'll bet you weren't thinking about the possible danger at all. What do you think might have happened if you found the cat?"

"I-I-I never gave it a thought. I assumed it had gone to its sleeping place. Jay and I were talking about what we saw."

"You can't make assumptions when you are dealing with a wild animal. You should know that by now. You endangered Jay as well as yourself. Once again you weren't paying attention to what you were doing."

"Yes sir, I do. I wasn't thinking. I promise I will think about what I plan to do before I do it," I say carefully.

"See that you do or you may not grow up to be an adult!"

Pa is right, I was careless when following the cougar tracks. Jay and I found Buster though.

At supper, Pa tells us that he will hunt down the cougar as well as get us a deer tomorrow. "I feel something is wrong with the cougar since it is coming so close to the house and it could attack one of us next!"

"Ellen, please get a list together of your needs from town. Doc, you, and Ed go to town for the day to purchase the needed items and visit folks."

"All right, Charles" Doc says. He will visit his daughter and Uncle Ed will visit friends and relatives while they are in town.

Pa will go hunting—alone. Pa always hunts alone to be sure there would be no accidental shootings.

CHAPTER 10

▼

PA GOES HUNTING

Monday is a beautiful day, not very cold, and bright and clear. We will walk to school today. Ruthie and I finish our chores, get ready for school, and eat our oatmeal breakfast. Ma gives Doc her short list of our needs at Eaten Brother's Market and some money to pay for the items. Pa gives the men their wage money that is due them.

Doc has a daughter and her family in town that he sometimes visits and helps with money or by doing work around their house.

"Please take care of Buster while we are at school, Ma." I plead.

"That won't be very difficult," Ma says, "He seems to be content to sleep by the stove."

As we are afoot and the path through the woods is useable, we take that route. Ruthie and I have to walk slowly so Mary can keep up. She is jabbering away behind us, talking to herself, talking about Buster, and asking a zillion questions.

In between answering Mary's questions, Ruthie and I discuss Billy and what should be done about him. "I'm just about fed-up with Billy's meanness," I announce. "I guess I need some help with what to do."

"Why don't you talk to Pa about Billy after school today? He needs help dressing the deer and Doc and Uncle Ed won't be back till dark most likely," Ruthie suggests.

"That is a good idea and today is as good a day as any," I say. "It is too bad there can't be some way Billy can go to high school in town. I know he wants to and he should be able to but his Pa wants him to stay on the family farm. He needs Billy for the work he can do because his brothers are too young to help out."

"Oh, is that what his problem is?" Ruthie asks.

"Yes, he doesn't like me because I get to go to school. He said I always get things my way and my life is too easy. Billy wants to go to high school so he can be a shopkeeper or a bookkeeper. Please don't say anything to him about what I have told you. I don't want him to know I have talked to anyone about him. I have enough trouble with him already," I say.

"No, I won't talk to him about it. But I think you should talk to Pa, he might have some idea of what could be done to help Billy," Ruthie again suggests.

"I will," I say as I brace myself for whatever Billy has up his sleeve for me today.

*   *   *   *

Ma packs a lunch for Pa and he gets his rifle down from its pegs over the kitchen door. The gun is a Trapdoor Springfield and belonged to Grandpa Lee. Eighteen seventy-three is the year it was made.

I long to be able to shoot it and someday I will. For now, it is much too heavy and powerful for me to handle. It weighs about eight and a half pounds and is fifty-three inches long. It shoots a heavy bullet and Pa said it would knock me right off my feet and onto my backside if I fired it.

Pa has told me the Trapdoor Springfield was at first made from the old War of the Rebellion 1865 Springfield, which is a muzzleloader. The Trapdoor Springfield is a breechloader and is the first of its kind.

I love to watch Pa clean and care for the gun whenever he has used it. Sometimes he takes it down off its pegs just for me to look at and admire.

The stock is made of walnut and it is a dark rich brown. The barrel and other metal parts of the gun are deep blue-black steel.

Pa keeps the bullets for the rifle on the top shelf of the pantry. They are way in the back to make them impossible for us children to reach. He put six bullets in the right pocket of his heavy coat to take hunting with him.

After Doc and Uncle Ed finish their chores, they take Toby and the small cutter to town. It is about a twenty-mile round trip and they will be gone most, if not all of the day.

We wave good-bye to Pa and ask him to be very careful as we leave for our walk to school. I wish I could go with him to hunt deer and the cat but know better than to ask.

Pa tells me later that he left the house with a feeling of dread in his heart. He hoped he would not see the big cat because he did not want to shoot it. It was a danger to his family, however, and it would be a danger to his valuable livestock. Better to get this unpleasantness over with and the sooner the better.

Wild Andy was happy to see him and was up to his old tricks of refusing the bit and tossing his head so it was hard to put on his bridle. Pa spoke gently to him and quickly harnessed him in spite of his tricks. They went to the equipment shed and picked up the small bobsled.

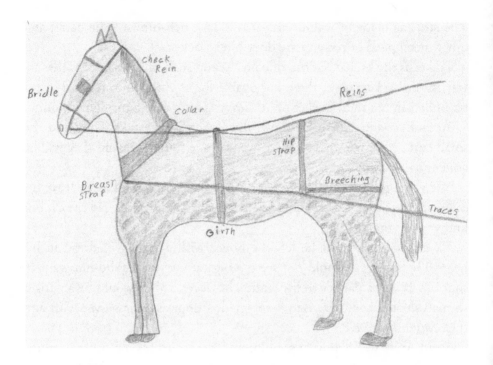

Pa checked the rifle again, put a bullet into the firing chamber, and pulled the hammer to the half-cocked position for safety. The gun would not fire unless the hammer was pulled all the way back. He slung the rifle over his back by its sling. He then clucked to Andy and used a firm tone of voice to urge him into a fast trot. Pa found great pleasure in flying along at such a speed. He loves beautiful animals, most especially a fine horse trotting in front of him.

Andy's mane and up held tail were flowing in the breeze. His ears pointed slightly forward, showing his eagerness to be on the way. Andy picked his feet up high displaying his pleasure at being able to trot so beautifully. It was his way of showing off.

As he got close to the woodlot, Pa slowed the horse to a walk and finally stopped. He tied the spirited animal to a tree using the lead line and went quietly into the woods on foot, gun at the ready.

His first duty was to find an adult male deer to shoot for food for his family. This time of year, December, the male deer would have antlers so it was easy to tell them from the does.

He looked for signs of the cougar as he quietly walked toward the ravine where he thought deer might be. He soon came across the herd and after studying them for a time, selected a large buck. He rested the barrel of the rifle against the trunk of a tree to steady it, pulled the hammer way back, took very careful aim, and fired.

Down went the deer! A clean shot! The other deer in the herd ran off in all directions in their panic. Pa went quickly to the downed animal and made sure it was dead. He field dressed the buck and began to drag the beautiful animal toward where he had left Andy and the bobsled.

Suddenly there was a horrible high-pitched scream! Only a panic-stricken horse could make a scream like that. Pa dropped the deer and began to run toward where he had left Andy. There was no doubt the horse was in some kind of trouble and the first thought that came to Pa's mind was that the cougar was nearby.

He came out of the woods about one hundred yards from the horse and could see Andy rearing and thrashing about. Wild Andy was in terror for his life!

The panicked horse continued screaming and lunging. Suddenly he was free! The rope he was tied with had broken. He was running as fast as he could go, bobsled, and all, away from the woods. There was a golden-tan cat streaking after him. No wonder poor Andy had panicked.

The cat was no match for Andy's galloping speed and the distance between them quickly widened.

Pa continued to run toward the spot where the horse had been in hopes of getting a shot at the cat.

Shoot the cat? He realized he had not reloaded his rifle after shooting the deer! He was running after a hungry cougar with an unloaded gun! How could he be so careless?

Pa stopped and with shaking hands and gasping breath thrust a bullet into the chamber. As he again looked ahead, there was the cat running right at him! He quickly lifted the gun to his shoulder and with no time to aim, fired! The animal let out a furious cry!

The next thing Pa knew he was on his back in the snow. There was a heavy weight on him and the smell of warm blood plus cat. A sharp pain struck his left thigh and chest when he struggled to free himself. His chest hurt where the butt of the rifle had hit him, driven there by the forward motion of the cat.

He knew he was safe, that the cat was dead, because it was not moving.

Gathering his strength, Pa rolled the cat off and sat up in the snow. At his feet lay a beautiful large, male cougar. It was a little thin looking and upon careful examination, Pa realized the cat had a badly injured hind leg.

Therefore, that was why it was hunting easy targets like small game, Buster, and tied up Wild Andy.

Pa examined his own leg and found only a long tear in his wool pants and under drawers and a painful but not deep cut in his leg where the cougar bit him. He was shaking all over and could not help but think of his near miss with death!

How foolish he had been not to have reloaded his rifle before coming out of the woods when he knew something was bothering Andy.

He field dressed the cat so it would be lighter to drag. Now how was he to get home? He had no horse, no bobsled, and his rifle, a deer and a cougar to carry.

He sat on the big cat to rest because he was still shaken by his experience. He decided to eat his lunch, as he was suddenly very hungry.

It was quite cloudy now and the sun was sinking in the west. It was late afternoon already. With any luck, Andy would run home and alert the folks that he was afoot. After eating, Pa picked up the remaining end of Andy's lead and walked into the woods to get the dead deer and finish dragging it out. Then he decided he would just start hoofing it for home, alternating dragging the deer and the cat. Therefore, that is what he did.

It was hard and painful work, walking for some ways pulling the deer, walking back to the cat, pulling it ahead and so forth again and again. He was making slow progress toward home and the sun was quickly sinking in its golden path to the west.

He was at the bottom of a small valley, with a little frozen stream meandering through it, when he decided to sit and rest before working his way up the hill on the other side. Pa sat on the cougar, which by this time was stiff and cold.

As he was sitting there, resting, he noticed movement on the rim above him and looked carefully into the darkening sky. There was someone there. He could just make out a small body on a horse. Pa quickly knew it was Danny sitting on a very nervous and jumpy Andy.

*   *   *   *

I look down into the dark little valley and see Pa waving at me. Boy, am I relieved! Pa seems all right! I wave back and try to keep Andy under control by speaking to him softly and patting him. Pa is shouting something but I can't quite understand. Andy is dancing around and snorting even more. I know that if he rears up I will fall right off his back.

Soon I realize Pa is telling me not to bring Andy any further. After sliding off, I tie him up short by his reins to a stout tree. He is still very jumpy and I'm glad to be off him. Pa is slowly walking toward me, I half run, and half slide through the deep snow down the hill to greet him.

"Pa, are you all right?" I shout.

"Yes, I'm sure glad to see you Danny! I was in quite a predicament! Where did you find Andy? Is he hurt anywhere? Is the bobsled wrecked?" Pa asks.

"Andy seems fine to me, just very nervous. Are you sure you are not hurt?" I ask.

"I'm all right, Danny. Thanks for coming to look for me. Where did you find Andy?"

"The three of us were walking home from school when we saw Andy trotting along dragging the wrecked bobsled. Ruthie and I managed to catch him just where the lane meets the path to the schoolhouse. He was very excited and it took us a few minutes to calm him down so we could unhitch what was left of the bobsled. We were very worried about what had happened to you."

"Can any of the bobsled be saved or is it finished?" Pa asks.

"It is pretty well wrecked but the runners and other metal parts can be used again. I think you will have to build a new one rather than fix the old one, Pa."

"Well, it couldn't be helped and I'm not surprised it is wrecked. The cat attacked Andy and no horse is going to stand still for that. The reason the cat was acting so strange is that it has an injured hind leg and couldn't catch a deer. Come and see," Pa says.

He leads the way back down into the valley and to the cat and deer.

"Take a look at the left hind leg," Pa says as we look down at the beautiful dead cat. "It has been chewed up by something."

"What about you, your coat is bloody and you are limping." A feeling of fear and concern comes over me.

"The blood is from the cat and I have a little scratch on my leg where the cat got me before it died," Pa explains. "It is nothing."

"That is a good sized deer," I say. "It will keep us and Uncle Jerome and Aunt Liz, fed for quite awhile."

"Yes, I hated to shoot him but a venison roast will taste pretty good."

"Continue with your story of how you got here, Danny."

"Not much else to say. Ruthie continued home with Mary and she is going to follow along toward the woodlot on Bess with a barn lantern. I stood on the side of the bob sled and got on Andy and here I'm."

"You did well to be able to ride him. Andy must have been quite excited," Pa remarks.

"He had calmed down some and wasn't too hard to handle until we got near here. Then he must have been able to smell the cat. That is when I saw you and got off him. He is tied up short and should be safe."

"It must have been hard for you to ride out when it was getting dark," Pa says quietly.

Pa knows about my fear of the dark.

"I was sure I would find you before too long, Pa. Besides, it wasn't totally dark yet and you needed me. I didn't give it any thought."

"Good boy! In any case, you showed great responsibility and good judgment by coming here to help me."

"Thanks Pa, I'm glad you are not hurt."

"Now we have to start for home. Andy isn't going to stand for being too near this cat but maybe we can put the deer on his back and tie it there with my suspenders. Let's give it a try," Pa says. He takes off his coat and I hold it while he unbuttons and removes his suspenders.

We pull the deer to Andy and while I try to keep him calm Pa places the deer on the horse's back and ties it to the harness. Andy is not very pleased about this situation and keeps looking at his burden with wide-open eyes and laid-down ears. He throws in a few snorts too.

I do my best to keep him quiet, while Pa checks him all over to make sure the cat or his wild run had not injured him.

"I'm going to remove unneeded parts of the harness to make a line to have Andy tow the cougar. If we can keep him calm enough that is," Pa adds. "Let's drag the cat up and give it a try."

We walk back down into the valley and Pa and I pull the cat up the hill. I go ahead to try to keep Andy quiet as we get close to the horse.

Pa slowly walks ahead with the cat and talks soothingly to the horse. The smell of the dead cat, deer, and blood is more than Andy will take. He tries to get away and I cannot hold him. He is jerking me right off my feet as he rears!

Pa holds Andy's head while I tie the hind legs of the cat to the towline and use the lead line snap to attach it to the breast collar on Andy's harness. Pa had made a loop by tying a bowline and it made it easy to fasten the cat to the towline.

Pa says, "I'll give you a boost onto the horse."

"Don't you think you should ride Andy? Your leg must hurt you some and you would have better control over him, wouldn't you? There isn't room for the deer, you and me, is there?"

"That is a good idea, son; I'm a little worn out too. Ruthie should be along soon with Bess and you can ride with her. Let's get started for we have a long way to go."

After untying the reins from the tree, Pa gets up on Andy. I can see that his leg is hurting him and that he is glad to be off it. Pa turns Andy toward home and we slowly make our way in the dark. The horse is behaving itself now that Pa is in charge. I walk along behind to make sure we don't lose the cat.

We are moving along the edge of the dark woods, which is to our left. There is an open field to the right.

Even with Pa, there in front of me the strange shapes of the trees in the darkness make me feel afraid and uneasy! They sometimes look like wild animals or some fantastic creature from a bad dream. Behind me is nothing but darkness. I try not to but I just have to keep looking behind me, afraid I will find something there.

Slowly, I'm working myself into a panic. The wind is blowing the branches about and causing strange noises too.

What a scardy-cat I say to myself. The fear of the unknown is getting the better of me. I look up at Pa's big form sitting on Andy and feel better. I could not admit to anyone except Pa that I'm afraid of the dark! From then on, I concentrate on thinking of Pa and not the shapes in the woods and not what might be behind me.

After awhile Pa shouts, "I see a light ahead; it must be Ruth and Bess."

"That is good news," I reply. I'm getting a little tired of walking through the deep snow but don't want to admit it.

"Hello Pa, are you all right? We are all concerned about you. Where is Danny? I don't see him." Ruthie shouts.

"I'm all right, Ruthie, just a scratch. Thanks for riding out to help."

"I'm right here," I call. "What took you so long?"

"I got here as fast as I could," Ruthie explains. "Are you cold? I brought blankets."

"Don't bring Bess any closer, we have the cougar tied on behind Andy and she might be hard to handle," Pa orders.

"All right, I understand," Ruthie says.

I walk up to Bess and Ruthie and get a blanket for Pa. Even usually calm Bess has a wild, terrified look in her eyes.

"Take Bess' lead and use it to double tie the cougar to Andy so we won't have to worry about losing it, Danny. Then climb aboard Bess."

"Yes, Pa."

After I finish, I get aboard, wrap up in a blanket with Ruthie, and hold the lantern for her as we slowly lead the way home. It is some parade, big draft horse, light wagon horse, and dead cougar.

It sure is comforting to see the yellow glow of the lantern, on the snow around us. However, the bobbing, moving light makes very strange shapes in the woods. I try not to look in that direction.

I whisper to Ruthie that I think something is wrong with Pa that he is hurt more than he led us to believe. She doesn't know what to say. We never saw our Pa hurt!

We finally come across the damaged bobsled and Pa can only shake his head in dismay.

About this time, we can hear sleigh bells and then see a light and know Doc and Uncle Ed are coming to look for us in the small cutter. They want to make sure we are all right before they return to the house and to the rest of the anxiously waiting family.

Uncle Ed walks over to Pa and speaks quietly to him for a moment. We all move on toward home. The lamp light from the kitchen window is never more welcome.

Ma meets us outside the woodshed door and lets out a little gasp as Doc and Uncle Ed help Pa off Andy's back. Ruthie and I just look with wide-open eyes and gaping mouths. Our Pa needs help getting off the horse and walking into the house! He really is hurt!

"Pa, Pa, what's wrong?" Mary cries as she picks up a sobbing Carolyn.

Ruthie and I huddle with the little girls but we need comforting ourselves.

Doc calls to us from the woodshed door, "Start the chores, I will be right out. Ed, please hang the deer and cat so nothing can get at them."

"Yes, Doc, we will get started right away," Ruthie says.

"Come on, Ruthie, let's do the horses first," I say as I start to lead Andy toward the barn. I'm very upset by Pa's injuries.

Ruthie brings along Bess and asks, "What do you think about Pa? What if he is hurt bad and dies?" she asks dramatically.

"Let's not jump to conclusions. Perhaps he isn't hurt that badly. Doc will tell us when he comes out."

Ruthie and I go about our usual efforts. I try not to think about Pa but the early death of Grandpa Lee keeps entering my mind.

Ruthie and I do all of the horse work so Doc and Uncle Ed can take care of the cows and do the milking without Pa. My sister and I have to put the horses one by one in Bess' box stall so we can use the ledge to stand on to remove the harness and groom them.

When Doc comes into the barn, we rush over to him, "How is Pa, is he hurt badly?"

"Na, he isn't bad hurt. He will be all right in a few days. He is just banged up some," he explains.

I'm relieved but want to see for myself.

After the four of us finish the chores, we file into the kitchen and find only Ma there.

"The girls are visiting your father," she says as she filters the milk. "I want them to see he is all right. You two can take yours and his supper up to him and visit. Send the little ones down and I will eat supper with them."

Buster is very glad to see me and I give him a big but gentle hug.

Ma says, "He has been eating and it seems he is getting much better."

"What about Pa?" Ruthie and I ask together.

"Oh, he gave me quite a fright but he will be all right in a few days. Here, take this tray with you."

Ruthie and I don't know what to expect when we go up stairs to see our Pa. We only have seen Pa and Ma in bed on Christmas morning where we all gathered before coming downstairs to see our presents. There he is, propped up on some pillows and glad to see us with his supper.

We help him with his food and listen to him explain, "My ribs hurt where the rifle stock hit them when the big cat landed on me. Nothing seems broken, just bruised. I will be fine in a few days. My scratched leg will heal in a few days too. I'm lucky it wasn't worse!"

"That is wonderful Pa," Ruthie exclaims. "We are so glad you were not hurt bad."

Ruthie continues, "You know the Marshall family that lives on the road past Uncle Jerome's place? Their son, Billy, has a personal problem and he is taking his unhappiness out on Danny at school. Danny doesn't know what to do. We are sure you will have some ideas. Go ahead Danny; tell Pa what you told me."

"Well, it seems Billy doesn't want to work on his Pa's farm. He wants to go to high school in town and be a shopkeeper or bookkeeper."

"He doesn't like me cause I get to go to school every day while his Pa only lets him go during the dead of winter. I would like to help him because he is a good student and he should be able to do what he wishes with his own life. He has younger brothers who can work on the farm but they are not old enough yet.

"Let me get this straight. Billy Marshall has it in for you. What is he doing to you?" Pa asks harshly. "Why didn't you say something before this?"

"Billy plays mean little tricks on me that sometimes get me in trouble with Miss Spaulding," I say.

"The other day he took a pen from one of the girls and put it on my desk to make it look like I had taken it. I feel that teacher knew I wouldn't steal someone's pen. But after she gave it back to the girl, she took me out to the cloakroom and asked me about it. I told her that I did not take it and that I didn't know how it got on my desk. I hope she believes me. I don't know what the girl might think. It all is very embarrassing."

"I wanted to take care of my problem with Billy by myself but haven't been unable to."

"Whose pen was it, Danny?" Ruthie asks.

"What difference does that make?" I ask sharply.

"It doesn't, I just want to know."

"It was Amelia's pen, you know, that special one she got for her birthday. Please, Pa, do you have any ideas that might help Billy to be able to do what he wants to with his own life?"

"You say he is good in school and wants to work in town and go to high school?" Pa asks.

"Yes, but I can't see how it can be done because his Pa needs him on the farm and does not want him to go to town to live."

"You know, my Cousin William Fenner might need an apprentice," Pa says thoughtfully. "The last time I spoke to him at his office in town he said he had more work than he knew what to do with and had to turn some people down. Perhaps some business arrangement could be made with him so Billy could work for him and go to high school and at the same time earn enough money for his Pa to be able to hire a boy to help him."

"Oh, Pa, do you think so?" I cry.

"I don't know for sure, I will have to talk to Cousin William first and if he is agreeable. Then we will have to talk to Mr. Marshall and Billy. The boy will have to be willing to work hard to get what he wants. It will take some arranging but it will be worth trying, don't you think?" Pa asks.

"Oh, yes, Pa, it sounds like just what Billy wants," I say. "Thanks for understanding and offering to help. I won't say anything to Billy until after you speak to Cousin William."

"You are more than welcome, Danny. Everyone deserves to have a chance to do what they want with their life. The next time I go to town I will speak to Cousin William."

"You know you and your big sister will have to help more in the barns with the chores until I'm on my feet again," Pa says.

"Oh yes, Pa, we will," Ruthie speaks for both of us as usual.

CHAPTER 11

▼

BILLY AND DANNY

It is Saturday and Pa is up and around. He is going to take Ma into town after morning chores. Buster is his old self too. He sure looks funny with his cut off fur though.

Christmas is only a week away and our Ma and Pa want to get some shopping done. Pa also is taking a load of dry red beans to Mr. Stark to sell and Ma has a few pounds of butter and some eggs to sell at The A & P Store. The price for the butter is eighteen cents a pound and the eggs for twelve cents a dozen.

Any of us who had the time were part of the work to get the beans ready to sell. They had been machine thrashed but could use more work. This means picking over pound after pound, bag after bag of beans to clean them. Before Pa sells the beans, we remove small stones, clumps of dirt, split beans, and pieces of bean vine. We sell the beans by the bushel and Pa would not cheat anyone by having non-bean material included. It just would not be honest.

Pa, Doc, Uncle Ed, and sometimes even Ma and we children sat on the upper floor of the cow barn on barrels and crates picking over the beans. Pa is paid $1.70 per bushel for his bean crop and he has thirty bushels to sell at this time. Some of this money we will use for Christmas presents.

Ma and Pa are using the lumber bobsled to take to town because the bagged beans are a large and heavy load.

My parents are stopping by Uncle Henry's farm to pick up Uncle and Aunt to take them into Penn Yan with them. In past years, they could have taken a steamboat to town but this year, with the early severe cold, ice has formed on the lake at Penn Yan. The lake steamers are no longer in use. It is going to be a long hard winter if the start is any indication.

Uncle Henry has red beans to sell too. Ma and Aunt Mertie can sit on the bags of beans while Pa and his brother take turns driving the team of Big Jim and Big Dan. They bring potato crates to sit on the way home.

When they got to town, Ma and Pa went to Mr. Wagener's Shoe Store and purchased shoes and rubbers for Ma for $2.90. He bought a pair of shoes for Uncle Ed for $3.00. Pa also discussed with Mr. Wagener the possibility of making shoe ice skates for Ruthie. Mr. Wagener, Pa later told me, said he would be glad to do it and they will be ready in a few days.

I decide to go for a ride on Bess and before she left Ma asked me to take some venison and other supplies to Uncle Jerome and Aunt Liz. Ma wrapped some butter, flour, elderberry jam, chops, stew meat, and a roast into several packages for me to carry. The butter is in a heavy crock with a clamp-on lid.

"Now remember, Danny, you are to be home long before dark," Ma instructs. "Promise me that you will be careful."

"Yes, Ma, I promise I will be careful and will be home long before dark."

After Ma and Pa leave for town, I harness Bess and slowly ride her along the road to the lake and Uncle Jerome's place. The food I carry in two gunnysacks tied together and slung over Bess' back in front of me.

Buster is tagging along with us. Sometimes he runs ahead as if to check the road. He runs back to Bess and barks once to tell us to hurry up. His tail is wagging a mile a minute. He sure is enjoying himself and is glad to do some exploring. He checks each new smell he finds. Bess is enjoying her relative freedom too.

It is a beautiful day, bright sunshine and only a slight breeze out of the north. The lake is the most wonderful shade of blue with little ripples on it. There are almost no clouds and what are there are the big, white puffy ones. I can see one very large cloud, south over the lake, edged in gold from the rays of the sun. What a day to be riding horseback and looking at nature at its best.

When I arrive at Uncle Jerome's barn, I put Bess in an empty box stall and give her some water and hay.

Aunt and Uncle are glad to receive the venison and other supplies. I stay at Uncle Jerome's place for a while to visit and bring in wood for them. We enjoy some johnnycake with butter and molasses on it and a hot cup of tea in their warm kitchen.

"Tell me more about your war experiences," I beg.

"Well, many of the men were surprised to find I had the same last name as the Reb General Robert Lee. Some even thought I was a Reb spy. I explained my family came from New York State and New England, not Virginia."

"Was it hard to become a soldier?"

"Not really, but, Danny, the army sure wants things done their way. It was hard not to laugh at my sergeant sometimes. I had been hunting for many years but still had to learn to use the army rifle the way they wanted. I was amazed at the number of men who did not know how to shoot. The sergeant asked me to help some of those who were having trouble learning."

"My sergeant also wanted to teach me to handle a team of mules. A bunch of us farm fellows got together and held a little parade of our own. We showed the army how to handle a team. It was great fun. The sergeant didn't take it too well though."

"What did he do?" I asked in surprise.

"He wanted to put us all on report. Our corporal, who had been a part of our scheme, explained things to him. Our sergeant got a good laugh then too."

"Most of the time we had fine experiences while in training. The boys who got sick were the exception. Some of them died long before we saw any Rebs! Those were sad days!"

After having dinner with Aunt and Uncle I leave early in the afternoon to make my way home. This would give me plenty of time to get home long before dark.

I decide I will ride to the schoolhouse and then take the woods path to home. As I near the schoolyard, I can't believe my eyes, there is a black and white Holstein dairy cow.

"What are you doing loose?" I ask. "Who do you belong to?" I know it isn't one of ours. We have Guernsey's which are white with reddish spots. The cow just looks at me with her big black sad eyes.

The nearest place around, other than ours, is Mr. Marshall's. Perhaps the cow came from there. If I can catch it, I can put Bess' lead around its neck and lead it home to Mr. Marshall.

I slide off Bess and tie her to a tree by her reins. After unsnapping her lead line, I set out to capture the cow. This is no easy task for she has developed a taste for freedom and isn't about to be caught.

"Buster, bring the cow," I call softly. Buster chases her toward me as Doc trained him to do.

The cow will get just so close and then off she goes galloping at top speed, bawling, full udder swinging and tail curled up in the air. She dodges about too, first in one direction and then another. Then she trots along, pleased with herself that she has evaded capture and just ignores a frustrated Buster. I become more and more disgusted.

Now we are over in the woods behind the school and I can see she is finally getting tired of this game. So am I. I call softly to her, "Here Bossy, here Bossy. See what I have for you!"

I do my best to sneak up to her while pretending I have something for her to eat. Buster is just sitting in the snow, panting with his tongue hanging out. It is as if he is telling me to catch her without him because he has given up.

Suddenly she stops running and allows me to walk right up to her and put the rope around her neck.

"What has gotten into you? After all this running you just gave up." She is a wise old cow after all.

A voice from nowhere speaks, "Hello, Danny."

I about jump out of my skin at the sound, but quickly realize it is Billy. Where is he? Then, there he is, sitting on an old oak tree stump looking as if he is glad to see me.

"Oh, hello, Billy, is this your cow?" I ask.

"Yes she is and many thanks for catching her for me. She had run off last night and I have been tracking her for quite sometime. She got away from my little brother Nelson when he was taking her to water. He didn't tell anyone and she had quite a start on me."

"You have been very difficult to catch, Clover."

Buster investigates Billy and finding him someone he knows, again sits down to rest.

Billy stands and I can see him wince.

"What's wrong? Are you hurt?" I ask.

"I hurt my ankle chasing this darn cow. It is very swollen and I can hardly walk on it. But I will make it home all right."

"I will be glad to give you a ride, Bess is tied over in the schoolyard," I offer.

"No, that's all right, why would you want to help me after all the mean little tricks I have played on you at school?" Billy speaks with his usual scowl on his face. "Did you like the dead flies in your lunch sack?"

"Well, that is what neighbors are for and that is the country way of doing things. When someone needs help, you offer to help them. Isn't that what your family does?" I ask. "The flies didn't bother me much. I got rid of them before I ate my lunch."

"Yes, but I have been giving you a really hard time and you shouldn't want to help me."

"That is not the way I have been taught to do things. When you find someone, who needs your help you offer to help no matter who they are. Do you want a ride or not?" I ask, getting somewhat angry. I can feel my face getting hot.

"Yes, I guess I could use some help about now," Billy replies with a smile.

"All right, stay here and hold on to Clover. I'll be back with Bess. It may take a little while because she is so big I will have to follow a round-about way."

I set off by the most direct route to the schoolyard. After untying Bess, I lead her into the woods. She walks obediently behind me and I have to take care that she has enough room to get between trees and under limbs. I finally arrive back at the spot where I left Billy.

After taking the rope for the cow, I help Billy, with the aid of the stump, onto Bess' back.

"You will have to lay flat up there until we get back on the road so you won't be hit by a tree limb. Here, take Clover's rope."

"All right, Danny thanks. This sure is a big horse but it beats walking with a sore leg. Lead the way."

I walk back toward the schoolyard but this time can follow my tracks in the snow and we get there in a few minutes.

"Move back, I tell Billy, I'm coming up." He begins to laugh at the way I have to climb up on Bess using the rope ladder, but stops laughing quickly.

We start on our slow way to Billy's house with the cow in tow. Clover is showing her displeasure by pulling back on the rope, shaking her head, rolling her big dark eyes, and occasionally bawling as only an upset cow can do. When she balks too much, Buster runs up behind her and gives her a little nip on a hind leg. That gets her started again.

Bess just continues to plod along, ignoring the cow completely.

The stately horse carries us down Mr. Marshall's lane and we stop by the house. Billy's Ma comes out and is glad to see us because she wondered why Billy hadn't found the cow and gotten home long before now. She was getting worried about him.

"Billy, are you all right? You were gone a long time. Where did you find Clover?"

"Over by the school yard, actually, Danny caught her. I hurt my ankle and Danny helped me get home.

"Thank you for helping Billy, Danny."

"You are welcome, Mrs. Marshall. I didn't do much."

After tying up the cow and Bess, I help Billy into the house and his Ma gives us a hot cup of tea and some oatmeal cookies. She even gives Buster some water and a crust of bread to eat. She is a pleasant woman and thanks me again for helping with the cow.

Shortly, Mr. Marshall comes into the house after putting Clover where she belongs. He has a scowl on his face but it turns to a smile when he sees Billy is home safely. Mr. Marshall asks what happened to Buster. He could see his healed wounds and areas of missing fur. I tell him about the cougar.

"Mighty dangerous thing, having a big cat come near the barns like that. Never know what a cat might do to livestock or people."

"Thanks for helping with the cow Danny. Clover has always been quite a troublemaker but she gives a lot of milk. Has a mind of her own that is for sure. Much obliged to you for helping us."

"That's all right Mr. Marshall, glad to do it. I must be getting home because my folks will wonder where I am."

They all put on their coats and come out to where Bess is standing, even the little children. Mr. Marshall helps me up so I do not have to use the ladder and thanks me again.

"You are welcome, Mr. Marshall," I say. "See you at school on Monday, and I hope your ankle is better soon, Billy. Good-bye everyone and Merry Christmas! Giddyap Bess, let's go home."

I urge Bess into a trot after we start down the lane. Her big hooves make a drumming sound on the hard packed snow as we speed along. I'm going to be very late getting home. Buster is bounding alongside the big horse, happy to be moving again.

CHAPTER 12

▼

CHRISTMAS SHOPPING

When I arrive home, I go directly to the horse barn, water Bess, and unharness her. I rub her down and clean the packed snow and ice from her hooves. I talk to her as I work, telling her about school.

"You remember my telling you how mean Billy Marshall sometimes is to me at school? Well, today when you and I helped him really came as a surprise to him. Billy didn't think I would want to help him but we showed him a thing or two about how to act! I do hope he can accomplish his goals."

Bess moves her ears back and forth, as I speak. She is a good listener. I give her a big hug and an extra pat on the nose. As soon as I finish, I walk to the house. Ruthie greets me at the door of the woodshed.

"Where have you been? I'm going to tell Ma and Pa how long you were away today. You were told to come right back from Uncle Jerome and Aunt Liz's place, why didn't you?"

Before I have a chance to reply, she continues, "You are going to get a spanking for sure for not doing what you were told and it is only a few days before Christmas!"

"I was not told to come right back from Uncle Jerome's. Ma told to be home long before dark. Well, it isn't even close to dark. It is just starting to get dark. You are yelling at me for nothing," I exclaim.

"Oh, ummmm, oh, all right then. But you sure were gone a long time and the sun is starting to set."

I tell Ruthie about Billy, the cow, and visiting the Marshall place. That quiets her outcries. Still, I'm glad I made it home before Ma and Pa.

Ruthie, Doc, Uncle Ed, and I begin the evening chores and by the time we finish Ma and Pa are home from town. Pa and I take care of Jim and Dan and I tell him all about my trip to see Uncle Jerome and Aunt Liz and helping Billy with his run away cow. I even tell him what time I arrived home. Now Ruthie will not have anything to tattle about.

"I'm glad you helped Billy. It was the right thing to do even if Billy is troublesome and difficult to get along with."

"Pa, he was surprised that I was willing to help him."

"You showed him the right way to act and I'm proud of you."

"Thanks Pa, it wasn't much. I only did what I would want someone to do for me if I was the one in trouble."

Pa says, "I talked to Cousin William about Billy while I was in town. He said he would be glad to take the boy on as an apprentice as long as his father agreed. He would pay Billy enough money so Mr. Marshall could hire a boy to help him when need be. And, Billy could go to high school when Miss Spaulding gives him his eighth grade certificate."

"Now, all that is left is to get Mr. Marshall to agree with the plan," I say.

"I will go to his place and talk to him soon or perhaps I will see him at the school Christmas party."

"May I tell Billy when I see him at school?"

"Sure, Danny, but make it clear to him that it all depends upon what his father has to say about the plan. He must agree to the arrangements," Pa explains.

"Now let's go see what your Ma has fixed us for supper."

Billy came limping to school on Monday and while we are in the cloakroom, I tell him what my Pa had said.

"Wow that sounds great! It is just what I have been hoping for. If only my Pa will agree."

How wonderful it is to see Billy with a big smile on his face. He doesn't play any tricks on me today either, and he doesn't play any tricks on me Tuesday.

Christmas is on Saturday and Wednesday is our last day of school for the week. We had drawn names for gifts for our school Christmas Party that is on Thursday night and I drew Rachel's. Boy, did Ruthie have fun with that!

I hope Billy has given up playing dirty little tricks on me but I'm wrong for on Wednesday afternoon he did it again.

I'm working on my handwriting exercises and am trying very hard to write neatly in my penmanship book. Miss Spaulding is going to look at it when I finish and I want my page to be perfect.

Then disaster strikes. Billy walks between the desks toward the stove and he bumps my right arm sending the pen flying across the page.

"Yipe," I yell in surprise and jump out of my seat and right back down again. An unwanted line and a big blob of black ink blemish my otherwise neat page. I catch the pen before it drops onto my pants to make another inky blob there.

Boy, am I disgusted and angry. I jump to my feet and into the isle between the desks. My fists are clenched and ready to use.

Billy looks down at me with that awful smirk of his. "Sorry Danny, it was an accident," is all he says. Then he begins to walk away. He stops, turns around, and comes back to me. Quietly he says, "You weren't planning to use those little fists on me were you?" He laughs right out loud, "Ha, ha, ha."

The whole class is affected this time. Everyone is looking at me. My only chance to keep Billy from being mean to me is in the hands of his father.

"Boys, take your places immediately! Your disagreement is disrupting the whole room," Miss Spaulding says with a raised voice.

Billy doesn't say anything and returns to his seat.

"Sorry, Miss Spaulding," I say. Billy has gotten me in trouble again.

Of course, when we return home from school, Ruthie tells Ma about teacher correcting my behavior.

"Danny disrupted the whole class today," she blabs.

"Is that so? Fore shame! What were you doing, Danny?"

Before I can say anything, Ruthie says, "He was getting ready to fight Billy Marshall."

I say, "Teacher told us to go to our seats, and the whole thing was over. It won't happen again."

Ma shakes her head and gives me a serious look.

I stare at Ruthie hoping my eyes are telling her to say no more.

We children have been making Christmas gifts for weeks. My wren house for Mary has an attached note saying I will hang it for her in the spring. I stained it dark brown and tried to paint pink flowers with green leaves on the sides but the results are more like pink blobs than flowers. I complain to Pa.

"It is the effort and thought that counts," Pa says. "I'm sure Mary will love it. You can't expect to make a perfect birdhouse when you have had so little wood working experience. It looks to me like you did a good job."

"Thanks Pa. It could be a lot nicer."

My gift for Carolyn turns out a little better. I carved a doll out of cedar. The results are not acceptable to me but Ma, Pa, Ruthie, and Mary told me it isn't bad for my first carving efforts. It smells good and I had fun being with Pa as he was showing me how to carve. I painted a face, hands, and shoes on it.

Ruthie is making a little dress and bonnet for the doll. She is also knitting a fancy white shawl for Ma.

Pa is taking Ruthie, Mary and me to town so we can buy presents on Thursday morning. We have the small cutter and Toby. Pa has put both sets of bells on Toby's harness so we sound very musical and Christmas like. We start out for Penn Yan right after breakfast. Pa says he will get some tobacco for Doc for his present and a ball for Carolyn.

We jingle our way down Elm Street when we enter town and go directly to Feagles' Meat Market. Doc and Pa had killed and dressed twelve chickens and twenty turkeys yesterday for the holiday market. Today Pa is bringing them into Penn Yan to sell.

"Good morning to you George, I have the dressed chickens and turkeys we agreed upon last week," Pa says to Mr. Feagles.

Mr. Feagles replies, "Good morning to you, Charles. Please put them on the scales and we will settle up. That is twelve cents per pound for the turkeys and eight cents per pound for the chickens."

"Yes, that is what we agreed upon, George."

"Merry Christmas!" I call to Mr. Feagles as I walk into his store.

"Merry Christmas to you, Danny, and to your whole family."

"Thank you, Mr. Feagles, likewise to your family," I say as I make my way to the meat scale with a wrapped turkey in my arms.

Pa and I carry the bundles into the store and place first the turkeys and then the chickens on the scales. After they are weighed, we put them into the store's cold room.

I don't want to think about what is inside the packages but know selling meat is one of the few ways Pa has to make money. It doesn't make me feel any better to know Ruthie and I will have fewer chickens and turkeys to take care of for a while.

Some families in Penn Yan will be enjoying Christmas dinner centered around one of our roasted chickens or turkeys.

After we leave the meat market, Pa gives each of us the Christmas money we are to have for our gift purchases. It comes from selling our poultry.

We drive to Hoban's Hitching Barn to leave Toby and the sleigh.

"Good morning to you Owen. How is the family?" Pa asks while shaking Mr. Hoban's hand.

Mr. Hoban replies, "They are just fine and all are in a dither about Christmas. How are your folks out on the Bluff?"

"Everyone is well and happy, thank you for asking. The children and I have come to town to do our Christmas shopping."

"Hello, children. Are you excited about Christmas?" Mr. Hoban asks with a smile.

We answer as a chorus of three, "Oh, yes, sir!"

"I trust you have been behaving and will find some nice things in your stockings come Christmas morning."

"Oh, yes, sir, very well behaved!" we exclaim.

"You have a good time doing your shopping, children," finishes Mr. Hoban.

Toby goes willingly into a stall after Pa and I unhitch the cutter, Pa puts a blanket over him. Mr. Hoban gives him a pail of water.

"I will give him some oats and more water around noon," Mr. Hoban says.

"Thanks, Owen," Pa says, and we walk down Maiden Lane toward Main Street.

"I will meet you three at Mr. Fenner's office on Jacob Street at noon. We will all go to the Benham House for dinner," Pa tells us. "Have a good time shopping."

"All right Pa," my big sister says as Mary and I nod our heads in agreement.

Mary and I are putting our money together to buy the shoe ice skates for Ruthie. We are to pick them up at the Wagener Brothers Shoe Store. Pa gave us a bit more money for this as we didn't have quite enough.

I was going to get a locket for Rachel but Ma said it was too personal so I decide to buy her some fancy hair ribbons. Ruthie told me she would help me pick some out that will go well with Rachel's dresses.

Mary says she wants to get my present at the A & P Tea Store so we go there first.

I run over to the shoe store to get the ice skates while Ruthie is helping Mary make her purchases.

This is the first time Mary has been shopping without Ma or Pa to help her. She is a bundle of nervous excitement. Her voice is more squeaky than usual and she is talking a mile a minute.

When I arrive at the shoe store, Mr. Wagener is standing behind the counter near the big brass cash register.

"Hello, Mr. Wagener. I have come to pick up my sister's ice skates."

Mr. Wagener is the great-grandson of the founder of Penn Yan.

"Yes, Danny, they are right here. My best workman made them special for your sister. I have them wrapped in some nice red paper. I'm sure your sister will like them."

"Thank you, Mr. Wagener," I say as I give him the money for the skates. "They will be a pleasant surprise Christmas morning. My sister skates very well and these shoe skates will help her do even better."

"You are welcome, Danny and thank you," Mr. Wagener replies. "Merry Christmas to you and your family."

"Thank you, sir, Merry Christmas to you, and your family."

I leave the shoe store and make my way through the crowded streets to the A & P Store. There are many people in town doing their Christmas shopping.

I cannot imagine what Mary is buying for me at the A & P Store but it must be something to eat and that sounds good to me.

A big part of the enjoyment of giving and receiving Christmas presents is the surprise. It is sometimes difficult for me to keep the secrets I know but I don't want to spoil the fun.

The girls are waiting for me outside the store when I get there. Mary has two small packages in her hands. I was hoping mine would have been something much bigger.

We carefully make our way across busy Main Street and go into Roenke & Rogers dry goods store in the Arcade Building.

The three of us are still trying to decide what we will give to Ma and Pa. I want to give Ma something that isn't practical like a fancy hair comb. The girls won and Mary and I combine most of our remaining money and buy Ma some light rose wool yarn so she can knit herself a sweater.

She often makes warm things for Pa and we would like her to make something for herself. Ruthie and Mary thought the light rose color would go well with Ma's Sunday dress, which is a medium brown. I didn't think it was right that she would have to knit the sweater for herself. We didn't have enough money to purchase a ready-made one.

For Pa we bought fabric for a new shirt. It is red plaid flannel. Ma has agreed to help Ruthie make the shirt after Christmas.

"Danny, please take Mary to the front of the store while I pick out her gift," Ruthie says.

"Come on, Mary, let's go."

Mary asks, "Do you know what she is getting for me? I want to know now. I don't want to have to wait till Christmas."

"Shush, you be quiet," I say. "You know you have to wait till Christmas so just forget about it for now."

"Oh, you're no fun. I'll bet you don't even know what she is buying for me."

"Do too, but I'm not telling you. You will just have to wait like the rest of us."

"I'll tell you what I bought for you if you tell me what Ruthie is buying for me," Mary says with a big grin on her face.

"Never mind! I'm not telling no matter what," I reply with determination.

"Pooh! You are no fun," Mary cries again.

Just then, Ruthie finds us and she has a small package with her. It is wrapped in red and green stripped paper. Poor Mary looks as though she is trying to see through the wrapping.

For Miss Spaulding we buy a pretty Christmas card and Ruthie picks out a nice fancy hankie to go with it. We look at the hair ribbon material but I don't see anything I really like.

"Let's go to Lown's and see what they have for hair ribbons," I suggest.

Ruthie asks in her best big sister voice, "Nothing here is good enough for Rachel?"

"Well, I just want to see what else is available. That is reasonable, isn't it? I don't have to buy the first thing I see do I?"

"I suppose not," Ruthie sighs.

Back across the street we go. When we get to the other side, I realize Mary isn't with us! Ruthie is ready to go into Lown's when I grab her coat sleeve. "Where is Mary?"

"She was with you. Didn't you take her hand when we crossed the street?"

"No, I thought you had her. Where is she? I don't find her here or across the street."

"She must still be in the store, come on," Ruthie says as she half drags me into the busy street.

Just then, a fancy cutter that is being pulled by a beautiful black horse slides across our path. The man driving the rig shakes his fist at us.

"You children look where you are going. You have frightened my horse," he shouts at us. Indeed the horse has broken into a run and the man has all he can do to slow it. I don't care about his horse; I just have to find Mary!

We rush into the Arcade Building and there, standing in front of a fancy doll display is Mary. Her face is pressed against the glass display case. I see she has been crying when she turns toward us. Ruthie grabs her by the arm and almost pulls her off her feet.

I put my hand on Ruthie's arm and say, "It is not her fault. We were not paying enough attention to her."

"You are right, Danny. Mary, I do wish you would try to keep up with us. Now, don't cry. I'm sorry I pulled your arm."

A frightened Mary cries. "Where did you two go? I couldn't see you anywhere and decided to stay put. That is what Ma said to do if I was ever lost." She starts to cry.

I put my arm around her and give her a big hug. "Please don't cry. Everything is fine now. Where is your hankie?"

"I don't have one," Mary says in a weak voice. "I forgot to get one."

"Here, you can use mine," I say as I pull it out of my back pocket.

"Thanks, Danny," she sniffs.

We again make our way across Main Street. This time Ruthie has one of Mary's hands and I have the other.

In Lown's I select some white ribbon with a little pink thread going through it and some brown ribbon with gold leaves woven in it. Ruthie and Mary agree these will look nice with Rachel's dresses and hair.

The clerk measures the lengths of ribbon I have selected and tells me it will be ten cents for both. I have just thirteen cents in my pocket. The clerk takes my two nickels, writes something on a small piece of paper, puts them in a small cup, and sends them flying across the room to the office using the overhead cable system.

The three of us stand there looking up fascinated by the machine. The little round car moves quickly after only a short pull on the spring device that activates it. A car comes flying back with my receipt and I watch it as it comes to a stop in front of me. The store clerk wraps my ribbon in pretty red and green print Christmas paper and gives me my receipt.

"Thank you for your purchase, young man," she says with a smile.

"You are welcome, ma'am," I reply and smile back at her.

"All right, where to now?" I ask Ruthie and Mary.

"I want to go to the Cornwell Book Store," Ruthie says.

"Me too," Mary adds.

"Danny, please stay outside the store so I can look at things for you. Mary, do you want to get your gift for Carolyn here?" Ruthie asks.

"Yes, I think so," Mary answers in her excited voice.

Into the store, the two girls go while I stand outside and admire the teams, single horses, and rigs as they go by. There are all kinds of rigs and horses. Draft horses pulling heavy bobsleds loaded with merchandise or produce to fancy trotting horses pulling very light cutters. It is fascinating to watch them go by. I could stand here for hours.

I try to decide what horse or team I like the best but it is impossible to do. I like all of them. Someday I will have a fancy team and cutter of my own. I just know it.

Finally, Ruthie gives me a poke with her elbow. "Come on, stop daydreaming. I have had enough shopping for now," Ruthie complains.

I notice each girl has another package. "Did you find what you wanted?"

I got some building blocks for Carolyn," Mary says.

Ruthie says, "I found something I think you will enjoy very much but I'm not going to tell you what it is."

"I can wait to Christmas, Ruthie." I really want to know now but know Ruthie would take great pleasure in hearing me beg. She wouldn't tell me anyway.

"Do either of you want me to carry some of your packages? I only have two."

"Yes, here, you can carry these two large ones from Rogers," Ruthie says as she pushes the packages into my arms. "I'll carry your small package for you. Let's find out what time it is."

We know where there is a big wall clock in a store that can be seen from the street. Ruthie looks in the window and tells us it is eleven-thirty.

"Oh, good," I exclaim. "Let's go to the candy store on the corner and get some candy. I have three cents left."

Mary's blue eyes sparkle with joy. "But, we aren't supposed to eat candy right before a meal," she reminds us.

"It is only one piece each, Mary. I don't think it will hurt us any. If you don't want to eat yours now, you can save it for later."

"Oh, I'll eat mine now," she says with a giggle and a smile.

It is off to the candy store where we select the flavor we want of the penny candy. Mary takes forever. I give the clerk my three cents and we stand on the street corner of Main and Jacob enjoying our treat. I have cinnamon flavor.

I again enjoy looking at the horses as they prance by. Some of the teams have on ornate harness with lots of bells. These elegant rigs are pulling fancy cutters with fancy dressed people inside. I wonder who all these people are, where they live, and what they do to have such grand teams and sleighs. Our teams and rigs always look nice but they aren't very ornate.

"Ruthie, where do all these people come from?" Mary asks breathlessly.

"I guess most of them live here in town. Aren't some of the dresses really elegant?"

"Wouldn't you like to see their houses?" Mary asks.

"I sure do!"

"I wonder what they do for a living." I ask.

"Pa once told me there are some people here in town that don't even need to work because they have so much money," Ruthie says.

"Wow! I wonder how they manage that!" I say.

By this time, it is almost noon and we walk down Jacob Street to Mr. Fenner's office. We are very excited to eat dinner at the Benham House in a real dining room.

Ruthie says, "The food isn't as good as it is at home."

"I don't agree. Well, perhaps it isn't any better, just different," I say. We don't eat in town very often so it is a real delight for us to see the inside of the big fancy hotel and eat in the dining room.

Pa and Mr. Fenner are waiting for us inside his office. They put on their coats and hats after Mr. Fenner greets each one of us individually. I can see that Ruthie is enjoying the attention but little Mary is embarrassed by it. Her face is red and she does not know what to say to him. I myself do not know what to make of a man who does not farm for a living.

Mr. Fenner has on a splendid black suit and his black boots are shining like mirrors. I look at his hands as he is putting on his black leather gloves. They are white and soft looking. They aren't anything like my Pa's hands.

We children are on our best behavior, minding our manners and speaking only when spoken to.

Mr. Fenner is the husband of Ida Baker Fenner. The Baker family is related to Grandma Lee who had the last name of Baker before she married Grandpa Lee.

"You may leave your packages here, children," Mr. Fenner suggests. "We will come back here after we eat dinner."

A young lady, dressed in a dark blue outfit, takes the packages from us and puts them in a closet together with Pa's. I wonder what Pa bought.

We walk back to Main Street and the Benham House. We children walk a short distance behind Pa and Mr. Fenner. Several people greet the two men as if they know them well. I'm proud of my Pa, knowing all these people. His suit, coat, and hat are not as fancy as that of Mr. Fenner and his hands are rough and dirty looking. However, I'm proud to have him be my Pa.

Inside the Benham House, I must quietly remind Mary to shut her mouth. She is so excited by the sights she sees she doesn't know she has left it hanging open. Ruthie gives us a look of disgust. A man dressed in a fancy suit who knows Mr. Fenner escorts us to a table in the dining room. They call each other by name.

"Good afternoon, Mr. Fenner."

"Good afternoon, Frank. My usual table, please." Almost immediately, another man comes to our table. He is dressed in a different fancy suit. Mr. Fenner knows this man too.

"Welcome to my table, Mr. Fenner. Will you have any more guests?"

"No, I'm expecting no one else, Ralph."

Frank gives us each a menu and fills our water glasses. I have no idea what to order and look at Pa questioningly. Ruthie is looking at the menu as if she knows what she is doing and Mary is very unsure of what she is supposed to do.

Pa asks, "Do you children know what you would like to eat?"

Ruthie says, "I would like the roast beef and gravy, please Pa." She puts down her menu and places her hands on her lap.

I say, "I would like the chicken and biscuit if that would be all right, Pa." Mary gives me a light touch on my leg under the table. "I think Mary wants the same as I."

"Mary," Pa asks, "would you enjoy the chicken and biscuit?"

Little sister Mary nods and her face gets red again. She put her head down trying to hide her embarrassment. I take her menu and place her napkin on her lap.

When the waiter returns Pa orders for us children and orders a steak and mashed potatoes for himself. Mr. Fenner also orders the steak and mashed potatoes.

Pa tells us about some of his purchases while we are eating. Sometime ago he had ordered a hanging oil lamp for over the dining table from the Sears Roebuck catalog for Ma. The package had come by express and he is going to pick it up today. I also told us he had bought a big red ball for Carolyn.

The food is good but the biscuits are nothing like my Ma's. We children get through the whole meal without spilling any food on the white tablecloth, ourselves or dropping a piece of silverware on the floor. I know Mary is trying very hard to be good and so am I. Actually, I have been trying to be very good for so long I can hardly stand the strain any longer. Will Christmas ever get here?

After we finish eating, we walk Mr. Fenner back to his office and say good-bye to him wishing him and his family a very Merry Christmas. We pick up our packages and then continue down Jacob Street to visit the train station, one of our favorite sights in Penn Yan. No train is there so Pa checks with the ticket agent to see when the next train is due.

"There will not be a train for half an hour. Do you want to wait here or walk around?" Pa asks after speaking to the agent.

We vote to walk around and we walk down Hamilton Street all the way to Clinton Street admiring the houses and wondering who lives in them. Presently we hear the train whistle and make our way back to the station just in time to stand on the platform and watch the train come in.

"Oh, look, Pa!" I shout over the noise, "The engine has the same wheel arrangement as Jay's toy engine!" The engine comes to a stop right in front of us. It lets out a big white cloud of steam and black smoke.

"So it does, Danny."

We are amazed to see how many people get off the train and how many satchels, boxes, and bags they have with them.

Ruthie says, "It looks like a lot of people have come to Penn Yan to visit folks for Christmas. Mary, look at that little girl over there, she looks a lot like Carolyn."

Mary laughs and jumps up and down with amazement looking at the pretty, little girl who looks so much like our little sister. One glance from Pa makes her act better mannered.

The train only stays a few minutes and when the passengers who are leaving Penn Yan get on, the conductor signals the engineer, steps onto one of the slowly moving cars and the whole train noisily puffs away. It is not long before it is out of sight.

I cannot help but wonder where the people are going and where the people who had gotten off had come from. Someday I will go for a long train trip and find out some of these things for myself.

"Shall we pick up Toby and be on our way or do you have more shopping to do?" Pa asks. He has gotten his package from the express agent.

We agree we have had enough shopping to last us for a while and would be glad to be on our way home. We walk to the hitching shed and Mr. Hoban and Pa harness Toby and hitch him to our cutter. Pa pays Mr. Hoban ten cents for taking care of Toby. We place our packages in the covered box behind the seat. We pile in, say "good-bye" to Mr. Hoban, and wish him and his family Merry Christmas.

We get home just in time to do chores, eat a light supper, and get ready to go to the school Christmas Party. The house smells like gingerbread cookies so I know Ma and Carolyn had baked while we were away.

CHAPTER 13

▼

SCHOOL PARTY

Before we change into our dress up clothes, Ma looks us over to be sure we are clean and properly dressed for a party. I make extra effort to wash behind and in my ears and scrub my neck until it hurt, and pass inspection. I have even combed my hair without being told. Of course, the girls pass inspection.

Ma has on her brown dress and her gold chain and locket that Pa had given her on their first wedding anniversary. Pa looks splendid in his black suit and red vest.

Ruthie had knit the vest for Pa for Christmas last year. Ruthie's hair is neatly braided and the braids wound about her head. I have to admit she looks very mature. This will be her last Christmas Party in our little school house and I know she is sad about it.

The party is for anyone who is in the school and their parents. There is not enough room for very many people, especially adults. Little children who are not yet in school can come too.

Little Carolyn is glad to be included as she remembers from last year that there will be many good things to eat.

"Ma, can I eat all the cookies and candy that are offered to me?" she asks.

"No, you may not! It is time you start acting like a lady. Mind your manners and only take one thing to eat at a time. Eat slowly and be sure to say please and thank you. That goes for all of you children. Anyone that I see with more than one thing to eat at a time will have something removed from their Christmas stocking. Is this understood?"

"Also, please keep your voices down. I don't want to be able to hear any of you above the others. Do not speak to an adult unless you are spoken to. Please remember, everything you do says something about you, good or bad."

"Yes'm," we answer in a chorus. These are our usual visiting instructions. Pa is broadly grinning at us. I know he too is thinking of the good things we will have to eat.

Doc and Uncle Ed have hitched Toby and Andy to the big family cutter. The men gave the team an extra good brushing and have two strips of bells fastened to their harness. They look beautiful.

I wonder who has drawn my name for a Christmas gift. I try not to think about the present I will receive by thinking about my gift for Rachel. The ribbons I have chosen are very special to me and I hope she will think so too. I carry her package in my coat pocket so as not to tear the wrapping paper. On the outside is a little Christmas card that I have signed, Danny Lee.

Another thing I keep thinking about is the food. There will be so many good things to eat it will be very difficult to not make a pig of myself. I don't want Ma to have a reason for taking a gift from my Christmas stocking.

Ma made popcorn balls to bring and they are sitting in the center of the kitchen worktable. They are in a big blue metal kettle with a lid on top. I carry the kettle out to the cutter and hold it on my lap. Pa and I sit in the front and Ma and the girls are on the back seat.

It is a clear and not too cold night so the ride to the schoolhouse is a pleasure. The moon is just a little white sliver in the eastern sky but the stars are so bright we have enough light without using the lantern Pa has brought.

Carolyn whines, "Won't someone tell me about my presents?"

"No one will tell you and spoil the surprise on Christmas morning," Ma says. "And remember to act like a little lady at the party."

Some other sleighs or bobsleds and teams are already at the school when we arrive. Pa sees Mr. Marshall and directs our team next to his. Mr. Marshall is putting a blanket on each of his horses.

"Ellen, you and the children go in, I will be there directly," Pa says.

"All right children; let's see how the party committee has decorated this year."

"Ma, do you think there will be any ribbon candy?" Carolyn asks.

"Oh, I'm sure someone will have made some. We will find out soon."

Ruthie drew the name of one of the first graders and made a warm hat for her.

Mary had drawn Stan's name and had been at a loss as to what to buy for him.

I told her, "Get him something to eat and he will love it." I'm not sure what she did but she bought his present in the A & P Store too.

Carolyn does not have a gift to give and will not receive one. Ma explained to her she would be included next year when she will start first grade. I still have Rachel's gift in my coat pocket. I sure hope she likes it.

Ruthie opens the door because I have my hands full with the big kettle of popcorn balls. After hanging up our wraps, we walk into the brightly lit schoolroom. There are so many lamps that people have brought from their homes that it is just like a sunny day inside. I place the kettle on the table with the other food. What a large assortment of good things to eat!

The schoolroom is beautiful with red and green paper chains draped around the blackboards and framed pictures. The Christmas tree is standing on Miss Spaulding's desk in its place of honor. It is decorated with strings of popcorn and a few lit candles. Several pails of water are under the desk in case a candle sets the tree on fire.

The presents are under the tree and Ruthie, Mary and I place our gifts with them. I try to guess which one is mine but soon turn again to the food table. Wow! Everything looks so good! What should I eat first? Then I remember that Pa has not come into the school and wonder if he is talking to Mr. Marshall about Billy. I sneak outside to overhear the following conversation.

"Hello, Marshall. Nice night for the Christmas party."

"Yes, Lee. It is very pleasant indeed."

"I was talking to my cousin, William Fenner, in town the other day. He said he is looking for a boy to help him in his office. An apprentice in bookkeeping is what he said he was looking for. I thought of your Billy. He will be finishing the eighth grade this spring won't he?"

"Yes he will."

"My Danny has said your Billy is very good in his school work, especially arithmetic. Is there any chance he would like to go to work for Fenner?"

"I'm sure he would but I need him to help me with my farm work. I don't have the cash to hire a boy to replace him. I know he wants to work in town and I would like him to do what he wants with his life. However, I don't know how I would get my farm work done. My other sons are too small to be of much help."

"What if Fenner would pay Billy enough so you could hire someone to help you when you need? He told me he would be willing to pay the apprentice if he did a good job and worked hard."

"That sounds like it might work out. I would have to talk it over with Billy and then talk the situation over with Mr. Fenner the next time I go to town. Billy is a good and willing worker and I'm sure he would work hard for Mr. Fenner. You are a good neighbor Charles Lee and Billy and I are much obliged to you."

"Let's go inside and see what the ladies have brought for us to eat. My misses made her sugar cookies and even frosted them," Mr. Marshall says.

As Pa walks into the schoolroom with Mr. Marshall, I duck into a group of people. Pa gives me a quick smile and then a wink. I know Mr. Marshall has agreed to talk about Billy's apprenticeship to Mr. Fenner. A feeling of warmth spreads through my body. It sure is a good feeling to have been part of helping someone.

I can see Billy is looking at my Pa and his Pa to see if anything has been decided. When he sees a smile on his father's face, he knew arrangements might be worked out for him in town.

Most everyone has arrived at the party by now. Many of the adults are standing around the outside of the room. They are talking to neighbors they don't see much of in the winter. All of the students look like they are enjoying themselves and I look about for Stan to talk with. He is over by the food, of course.

I start to make my way through the crowd of people toward Stan when all of a sudden Amelia is standing in my way.

"Hello Danny. It is a wonderful night for a party, don't you think?"

"Amelia, what do you want? I mean, ahhh, err, you are right; it is a very nice night for a party."

"I brought you a little gift for Christmas and I want to give it to you now, here."

"Huh! Did you draw my name? Why don't you put it under the tree with the others?"

"No, I didn't draw your name; I just want to give you a little gift." She is slowly edging her way toward me and forcing me to move backward toward the wall. I can feel my face getting hot and know it is becoming red.

What does this girl want? Why does she want to give me a gift? I don't know what to do. There she is, standing before me with a thin package in her hand. The package is wrapped in red tissue paper. My back is to the wall now. I can go no further.

"What did you do that for? I don't have anything for you."

Amelia leans toward me and quietly says, "I just want to, Danny. Here, please take it."

"Uh-oh aaaammmm. Thanks, Amelia. Should I open it now or wait till I get home?" Amelia is gone; she is talking with some girls.

Rachel is looking right at me from across the room. Her eyes look like ice.

I jump out of my skin as Miss Spaulding asks, "Danny, would you please put this star on the top branch of the tree?"

"Yes, teacher, I will be glad to."

I'm saved! I take the little glass star and admire it for a moment. It is bright and shiny and always decorates the top of the school Christmas tree. The light of the candles on the tree and that of the oil lamps in the room are reflected in it a thousand different ways.

I try to place it on the upper most branch. I can't reach it. Once again, my lack of height is embarrassing and frustrating me. I can feel my face getting even redder.

Suddenly Billy is behind me and quickly puts the star in its place. He saves me from having to admit I cannot reach the top branch of the little tree. I give him a weak smile and he returns my smile with a big one of his own. Billy is a happy young man.

Teacher rings her little bell and the crowded room becomes quiet. "Mr. Brown has graciously agreed to play his accordion for us again this year. Let us sing some carols."

We sing *Hark, the Herald Angels Sing* and *O Little Town of Bethlehem*. The joy is gone for me. I can't even reach the top of the little Christmas tree. Ma works her way to my side and puts her arm around my shoulders. She noticed my failure and knows I'm upset. She gives me a hug and a squeeze and I feel a little better. We stand together to sing *Silent Night, Holy Night*.

We sing more carols and Mr. Brown makes a little speech. He is the district school superintendent. I want to eat not listen to talk.

Mr. Brown says, "I think we should all thank the decorations committee for their efforts in decorating the room. How nice it looks."

Everyone claps and looks around the room to find the women who are members of the decorations committee.

"We should also thank the ladies who brought the refreshments. How delicious everything looks!"

We clap again.

"Now I think we have waited long enough. Let us have a bite to eat."

We greet this with loud cheers.

I'm going to have more than a bite.

Carolyn is standing with me. "Remember what Ma said about only one item to eat at a time," I remind her and myself.

I start out with some chocolate cake and wash that down with a cup of hot-spiced cider. Next, I find some wintergreen ribbon candy. It is red and green striped with a white background. I give a big piece to Carolyn and we munch happily away together.

Then I eat a slice of apple pie with a dab of vanilla ice cream on top. It isn't as good as my Ma's but it is good. By the time I finish the pie I'm full but Stan comes by and gives me a chunk of fudge with walnuts in it. How can I refuse? I think to myself. I'm looking at the table and the remaining food when I realize Ma is glaring at me. Guess I have eaten enough, for now.

Miss Spaulding again rings her little bell and announces, "It is time for us to exchange gifts. Mr. Brown, would you please select a package from under the tree? I will read the child's name. The child will then be given the gift by the person who brought it."

After several student names are called, Miss Spaulding reads Ruthie's name. Little Sally Argyle stands up and slowly walks to the teacher's desk. She gives the package to Ruthie. White tissue paper covers the package. Ruthie carefully opens it and finds a small writing tablet.

"Thank you Sally, for the tablet. I will enjoy writing in it and I will think of you when I use it." Sally smiles a little and quickly goes back to her place by her parents.

Mary's name soon follows and she receives a package tied with a red bow. It is a booklet of paper dolls. Her blue eyes sparkle with pleasure. The blond girl who gave the gift gives Mary a hug and my sister hugs her in return.

Ruthie gives her package to little Nellie Grady. After she unwraps the bonnet, Nellie immediately tries it on. It looks very nice and everyone claps.

Then Mary gives Stan his gift. I watch closely hoping it will show me what she had purchased at the A & P store for me. It is a nice box of raisins. I hope she has gotten one for me too.

Rachel's name is next and I give her the package I have for her. She is not smiling. Then she sees the fancy hair ribbons and she looks pleased. She smiles at me and says, "Thank you." That is enough for me. I have put Amelia's package with my coat.

Finally, there is only one package left. It has to be for me as everyone else has his or hers. It is very small and wrapped in white paper. Billy stands up. Billy had drawn my name. He quickly hands me the little package.

Quietly he says, "It isn't much but I think you will like it." In the parcel is a little silver-colored metal whistle.

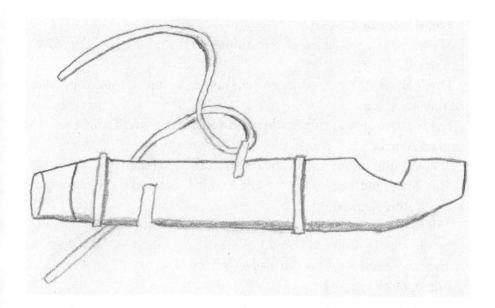

"Oh, thanks Billy. It is very nice and I don't have a metal whistle. I will carry it with me when I go riding."

"It plays several notes, not just one," Billy says.

"Oh, yes, I see. Thank you, it is grand."

"You are welcome, Danny. Thank you for helping me find a job in town."

"My pleasure, glad it worked out for you," I say.

How wonderful it is to be with a pleasant Billy!

We sing one more Christmas carol, *Glad Tidings of Great Joy I Bring to You and All Mankind.* Mr. Brown makes some closing remarks and the party is over.

I manage to get one last cookie without my Ma seeing me as we make our way to the cloakroom. I help Ma and the girls into the cutter. I have Ma's blue enameled kettle on my lap. It is empty of popcorn balls.

Ruthie looks at me with her piercing eyes. "What did Amelia give you? I saw her give you a Christmas gift. What is it?"

"I don't know, haven't opened it."

Why did Amelia give you a present?" Mary asks.

Because she wanted to, silly, she likes our brother." Ruthie says.

Oh, she does not," I say.

Well, why else would she give you a present?" Ruthie asks. "Your face is getting red."

Don't know." I try to get away from my sisters but Ruthie keeps asking me silly questions.

She is sweet on you that is why. Did you see the way Rachel looked at you and Amelia?"

"Look, I don't want to talk about this stuff," I say sharply.

"Let Mary and I see what the gift is and I won't ask any more questions," Ruthie suggests.

"All right here, you open it," I say as I hand the flat package to her.

By this time, I realize Ma is watching and listening to us. "Yes, open the package so we can see what Amelia has given to Danny."

I rip open the package.

"It is a print of a locomotive!" Ruthie exclaims. She must know how much you like the trains in Penn Yan."

"Yes, I talked to her about trains sometime ago. She likes them too and wants to take a train ride to some distant place," I say.

"How nice of her," Ma says.

"Rachel doesn't think so," Ruthie says.

"Are we ready to start for home?" Pa asks.

I'm glad to see him for it means I can sit in the front with my Pa and no longer have to listen to my sisters. We slowly make our way out of the schoolyard. There are several teams and cutters or bobsleds ahead of us. Toby and Andy wait to take their turn. Rachel and her family are nearby and I wave but she doesn't wave back. Maybe she didn't see me.

CHAPTER 14

▼

CHRISTMAS DAY

Christmas Eve day is finally here. We all are very busy wrapping our gifts. How do I wrap a birdhouse? Why do I select gifts I can't wrap? I moan to myself. Finally, after almost losing my temper I just put a big red bow on it. Ruthie tied the bow for me.

Mary and I didn't have to wrap Ruthie's skates as Mr. Wagener already wrapped them. I manage to wrap the little cedar doll in some red tissue paper.

"Children, please come down to the kitchen. Pa is going to crack walnuts for me and I need you to pick out the nutmeats. I'm going to make my maple walnut cake for Christmas," Ma calls up the back stairs. We had just done this with hickory nuts yesterday for Ruthie and Mary to make candy with.

An old sheet spread in the center of the kitchen floor makes clean-up easier. Pa is sitting on a chair in the center of the sheet. He has an old flat-iron between his knees and a hammer in his hand. There is a basket of this fall's walnuts on the floor next to him and a large bowl next to that. Clara is setting at his feet, waiting for the first walnut shells to go flying so she can bat at them with her front paws.

Ruthie, Mary, and I sit on the floor in a semicircle at Pa's feet. He begins to crack the hard shells and put them in the dish. One by one, we children pick out the nutmeats and put them in a small bowl. Ma starts to hum a Christmas carol and we join in.

Clara is dashing about after the flying shells. Carolyn is having fun watching and playing with Clara.

Presently, Pa asks, "How many of these do you need, Ellen?"

"About half the bowl full, please."

"We need a few more, Pa," Ruthie answers.

"All right, let's sing *Silent Night* and we will finish in no time."

It sure is pleasant to be sitting here on the floor with all the family gathered around. I wonder if other families are doing something like this.

Daniel, Uncle Jerome's son had come in his sleigh and gotten him and Aunt Liz to take them to his house in Rushville for Christmas. I know they are having a good family time too. Daniel has a wife and two small children.

Billy Marshall promised to take care of Uncle Jerome's livestock in the mornings. Uncle Ed will make the trip down to their place to take care of the animals in the afternoons. Billy is turning out to be a very nice fellow after all.

"Is there anything else we can do, Ma?" Ruthie asks as we finish the walnuts.

"You and Danny can go to the fruit cellar and pick out some of our best potatoes. We will need about thirty to make mashed potatoes for everyone at grandma's house."

"Yes, Ma, do you want anything else from down there?" I ask.

"No, nothing I can think of right now. Do you all have your gifts wrapped?"

"I don't," Mary wails.

"Do you want some help?" Ruthie asks. For once, she is smiling.

"Yes, please, Ruthie. I have tried and tried but it never looks right."

"I'll be glad to help you. Let's get the potatoes first, Danny."

Again, I resolve to buy or make only gifts that are easy to wrap. Ruthie is wrapping the materials we bought for Ma and Pa.

After we get the potatoes, I go back to my room and again bring out Amelia's gift to look at. I'm going to hang it on the wall next to my bed where I can easily see it. Why did she buy it for me? I don't understand why she would want to do such a thing. Ruthie gave me a hard time about it last night and even this morning but at last seems to have forgotten about Amelia's gift.

I admire my whistle again too and give it a few quiet toots. Billy must have given me such a nice gift to try to make amends for all the mean tricks he had played on me. I guess he will be a friend after all.

We have a light supper of soup and then make a big batch of popcorn. We sit in the family parlor eating popcorn and drinking hot-spiced cider. Pa is reading *A Visit From St. Nicholas*. Mary and Carolyn are playing with the paper dolls Mary received at the school Christmas party. We are all having a wonderful time.

Again, the thought comes over me how wonderful it is to have everyone so happy. How lucky I'm to have a loving family. Carolyn asks Pa to read the poem again and he pretends he doesn't want to. She sits on his lap and pulls on his suspenders until he relents and reads it again.

It is finally bedtime. We children go to our rooms so that Ma and Pa can hang and fill our stockings. They are hung from the old fireplace mantle in the parlor. The fireplace is closed off but the mantle is still there.

I can hear Carolyn and Mary jabbering away in the girls' room. I'll bet Ruthie wishes she could sleep elsewhere. Presently, Ma goes into their room and reminds the two little girls that St. Nick will not come if they are not asleep. They are quiet after that.

I can't get to sleep. I keep thinking about Amelia and Rachel. Why didn't Rachel wave good-bye to me after the school party? She looked at me but didn't smile.

Why did Amelia give me the locomotive picture? Finally, I feel myself falling to sleep.

It is Christmas morning at last! I can hear Ma, Pa and the girls talking. After putting on a heavy shirt over my nightshirt, I run into their room. We all get into their big bed, except Ruthie who must feel she is too mature for such a thing.

After our good morning hugs and kisses are over, we children hurry down stairs to see our Christmas stockings. Pa lights the oil lamp and adds wood to the parlor stove. He settles into his big chair to watch the fun.

Uncle Ed has joined us from his room in the bunkhouse. He has a small package with him.

First Carolyn receives her stocking. In it are wooden building blocks from Mary, a big red ball from Pa, my carved doll, a dress, and bonnet made by Ruthie for the doll, knitted hood and mittens from Ma, and an orange.

"Children," Ma says, "Doc has given each of us an orange. We gave him a dish filled with gingerbread men and hickory nut candy to take with him to his daughter's house in town."

"Oh, I love my gifts!" Carolyn exclaims. "Thanks Danny for the doll and thanks Ruthie for her dress and bonnet. Thanks Mary for the building blocks. Thanks Pa for the ball and thanks Ma for the hood and mittens. Oh, thanks to everyone." She runs to each of us and gives us a big hug and shows off her new toys and the hood and mittens. She then settles down to play on the floor at Ma's feet.

Now it is Mary's turn. She quickly grabs her Christmas stocking and dumps the contents onto the parlor floor. I give her the wren house, as it wouldn't fit in the stocking.

"Thank you Danny, it is wonderful!"

"You are welcome, Mary."

She quickly unwraps the package from Ruthie and finds a tiny china teacup and saucer. "Oh how pretty!" Mary exclaims. "These will look very lovely on the shelf in our room. Thank you big sister."

"You are welcome, Mary."

Carolyn had made Mary a necklace out of fancy buttons and she tries it on over her nightgown.

"Thank you Carolyn. I love my necklace."

Mary gives the little girl a big hug.

The hood and mittens Ma made for her are red and white to go with her red coat. "I love my matching hood and mittens. Thank you, Ma."

"You are very welcome, Mary," Ma says with a warm smile.

Ma had helped Carolyn make gingerbread men and one of those was in Mary's stocking too. It has raisins for eyes, nose, mouth, and buttons.

Pa hands Mary his present and she quickly tears off the tissue paper. It is a slate with her name written on the frame in fancy writing. No more will she have to remember to bring one home from school or use mine or Ruthie's slate.

"Thank you everyone for my wonderful presents," Mary says as she sits on Pa's lap and gives him a big hug.

"You are welcome, Sis. I hope you make good use of it."

"Oh, I will Pa."

I can see Mary really likes the little bird house as she has looked at it several times. I'm very glad I made it for her even if it was impossible for me to wrap.

"Danny, you may open your gifts now," Pa says.

My stocking is bulging it is so full. I'm so excited I want to hurry but at the same time I want to make my enjoyment last. I try to go slow, but not too slow. Right at the top is a beautifully carved locomotive! It is my gift from Pa. I examine it closely, admire the work, and give Pa a big hug and a "Thank you."

Ruthie hands me her gift. It is the book *Black Beauty*! It is a horse story. No wonder Ruthie had said she thought I would like it. I give Ruthie a hug and thank her.

Mary's gift is a box of peanuts—better than raisins. "Oh, thanks Mary, you remembered how much I like peanuts."

"Thanks Carolyn for the gingerbread man." I put my littlest sister on my lap and give her a little hug.

Doc's orange looks great. I'll have to remember to thank him when he returns from his daughter's house.

"Thanks Ma for my new hat and mittens." They are a bright blue and will be nice and warm.

Last is Ruthie's stocking. It is almost empty. We tell her that this is because she has been bad and doesn't deserve many gifts. In the stocking is some white lace for a dress collar and cuffs that Ma had tatted for her. The only other things are a gingerbread man and an orange. She looks a little disappointed and this makes it lots of fun to tease her.

"Ha ha, St. Nick knows you have been bad and didn't bring you much for Christmas," I tease.

Mary says, "You have been mean to us too often, Ruthie."

My big sister is looking at her mostly empty stocking with a puzzled look on her face. It is fun to be mean to Ruthie for a change.

Finally, I dash up the stairs to my room to get the box that contains the shoe ice skates. Mary and I hand her the box.

"Here Ruthie," I say, "This gift is from both of us." Ruthie is totally surprised and pleased by the gift. I can see it in her eyes.

"Oh, these will help my skating a good deal! Thank you very much."

Pa gives her his gift and we can't wait until she opens it. It is a book called, *Little Women*. How pleased she is.

"Thanks everyone for my gifts." She goes to each of us and gives us a kiss and a hug.

"I can't wait to try out the skates!" Ruthie exclaims.

She runs upstairs to get our gifts to Ma and Pa, which she had wrapped and kept in the girl's room.

Ma is very pleased with her white knit shawl and asks, "How long did you work on it? It must have taken you a very long time."

"Yes, it did at first," Ruthie says. "After I learned the pattern, it went along quite well. I'm glad you like it."

Ma admires the light rose yarn Mary and I had gotten for her. "I will start making the sweater right after Christmas. Thank you very much one and all."

"You are welcome," we say.

Pa also likes his flannel shirt fabric. "I will only wear the shirt in the house or going visiting as it will be too nice to wear for work."

Uncle Ed receives some gingerbread men and hickory nut candy. Pa gives him the new shoes. Uncle Ed has a set of double six dominoes for us.

"Children," he says, "these will help with your adding."

Thank you, Uncle Ed. Please help us learn how to play," Ruthie says.

Uncle gives us a smile and a nod.

We sit in the parlor and talk for a few minutes and then Pa gets up and goes out into the woodshed. He comes back with a big box that he puts on Ma's lap.

"Merry Christmas, Ellen," he says.

Ma carefully opens the box. The suspense is difficult to bear, as she is taking too long. We see it is a beautiful oil lamp.

"Oh how wonderful!" Ma says. "Thank you so much, Charles."

"You are welcome. We will all get pleasure from the lamp. It is to hang over the center of the dining table. We will have much better light when we eat and when you children do school work there," he says. "Ed and I can hang it before breakfast if you like. It won't take long."

Ma is really surprised by the gift, and pleased. "Oh, yes, please hang it as soon as you can. Let me get your gift, Charles," she says as she leaves the room. She comes back shortly with a nicely wrapped large package.

Slowly, Pa unwraps it and reveals a navy blue knit sweater.

"I hope it fits you properly, please try it on after you get dressed."

"It looks fine, Ellen. Thank you very much. I know how many hours of care and effort it took to make."

He gives her a big kiss right on the lips! And she kisses him back on the lips!

"I think we should all go and get dressed now," Ma directs.

"Wait," Mary hollers. "I have presents for Buster and Clara. They are family too." She skips to the pantry and comes back with a rag tied with a red bow. Dried catnip is inside for Clara and she has a chunk of rawhide for Buster. We let Buster in the house for the few minutes it takes him to eat his treat.

I dash upstairs and quickly get dressed in work clothes. Chores come before breakfast even on Christmas.

Ruthie and Mary take care of the poultry; I work with the pigs and Bess. Pa, Doc, and Uncle Ed milk and take care of the cows as usual.

The girls meet me in the horse barn.

"Danny and I will make breakfast. Come on Danny," Ruthie demands.

"I'll help too," Mary adds.

When we arrive at the kitchen Carolyn says, "I want to help too."

Uncle Ed says, "I'll get the tools to hang the lamp, Charles,"

Ma and Ruthie had made sweet rolls yesterday so Carolyn puts them on a platter. She also puts our oranges in a big bowl ready to go on the table after Pa and Uncle Ed finish hanging the lamp.

Ruthie and Mary make fried bacon and scrambled eggs while I make the coffee. The sweet rolls are on the shelf over the stove so they can warm. It is very pleasant to have Christmas breakfast by the light of the new oil lamp.

After breakfast, everyone is bustling about getting ready to go to Grandma and Grandpa Scott's house for Christmas dinner.

Uncle Ed and I go to the horse barn and harness Andy and Toby. I'm very careful not to soil my good clothes. We hitch the team of grays to the family cutter and Uncle lets me drive to the house.

Uncle Ed, Pa, and I carry out the eats and small gifts we are taking to Grandma and Grandpa's house and put them on the floor and front seat. The girls come out of the house and we pile into the sleigh. As we move out toward the Ridge Road Uncle Henry and his folks go by in their cutter.

"Pa, let's race them to Grandpa's house," I suggest.

"You know how your Ma would feel about that, Danny. We will have a race with Henry some other time. He has a good team there but they will be no match for our grays."

We slide and jingle into Grandpa's lane and pull up behind Uncle Henry's cutter next to the house.

"Ho, ho, ho," says Uncle Henry. "Christmas greetings to you all."

We reply, "Merry Christmas."

After helping the girls from the cutters, we carry the food into grandma's warm kitchen. Ma and the girls come in with presents for grandma and grandpa. Many greetings, and hugs and kisses are happily exchanged.

Pa, Uncle Ed, and I take our cutter over to the barn, unhitch, and unharness the team. Toby and Andy go into stalls next to Uncle Henry's team.

"Danny wants to have a race between your team and our grays this winter. How about setting it up sometime when the ladies aren't about?" Pa asks his brother.

"That is a good idea. We will have to do it sometime when they won't know about it. I know how Ellen would feel about our having a horse race. Mertie wouldn't like it either," Uncle Henry says firmly.

I'm eager to have the race today but know it can't be done. Ma would never allow a horse race on Christmas Day. We walk slowly to the house making plans for a race in the future.

As it is a bright, clear day, the view from the tip of the Bluff to the south is most dramatic. Pa has told me parts of four counties and two lakes are easy to see from this vantage point. To me it looks like the whole county is visible.

The slopes of the bluff look wonderful covered with snow. Many vineyards are here too. The Wagener Estate owns most of this land. Grandpa works some vineyards and farms some too.

Off to the west is a small grove of trees and among them is the large spring that brought the Indians and white settlers to the area. Jay and I have camped there. We love to play around the spring. We pretend we are Indians and have found arrowheads there.

Grandpa's house is built of stone and has walls almost two feet thick! It has four columns on the south side that go from the ground to the roof of the veranda.

Grandpa's blacksmith shop is located behind the house and to the west. It is great fun to help him when he is shoeing our horses or fixing a broken piece of metal farming equipment. He is a very small man, when compared to my Pa, as are all the Scotts. Grandpa is very strong though because it takes great strength to be a blacksmith. My Uncle John sometimes works with him in the blacksmith shop. Pa does too so he can learn about blacksmithing.

As we walk into the hall, Grandpa and Grandma and my aunts and uncles greet us again. All have on their finest clothes.

"Merry Christmas to one and all," Grandpa says in his Scottish brogue. "It is good that we are having this nice weather for the holiday. The women folk have been working very hard to cook delicious things for us to eat. I'll wager you and Jay can't wait a minute longer, Danny."

"That is for sure Grandpa. I can smell the turkey and the dressing."

I don't want to think about eating the fine animal. It was only yesterday that he was alive and strutting around in our poultry house. He was one of our largest toms.

The house is decorated for Christmas with holly, red candles, and sprigs of evergreen branches.

The Wagener Mansion is much more fancy then our place. The wood trim around the windows and doors is ornate with carving while ours is plain. The floors are made of varnished oak. Both the dining room and the parlor face toward the lake and its marvelous view. The windows there go from the floor to the ceiling.

The girls go to the dining room to finish setting the table.

Ma, Aunt Mertie and Grandma go down to the basement kitchen to check on the food and start cooking the potatoes we brought. The cookstove in the basement is in front of the huge brick fireplace, which is no longer used. The family lives much of the time in this big kitchen in the winter, as it is the warmest place in the house. The south walls of the basement face out toward Keuka Lake and so have a wonderful view.

We men folk gather in the parlor and wait to be called to dinner. There are enough women folk around so I don't need to worry about being assigned kitchen duty. Jay and I play with the yo-yo he received for Christmas and my locomotive. Carolyn is playing on the floor with cousins Warren and Aldy.

Finally, the awaited moment arrives and we all file into the large dining room. The small children are at a side table with Aunt Mertie to oversee their table manners. It was just last year I graduated to the main table with the adults.

We take our places and there, placed in front of grandpa is the big roasted turkey. I can't help but think about him when he was displaying himself around the yard with the other turkeys all proud and happy.

When my plate is filled with food, I conveniently forget about the turkey when he was alive. Everything looks and smells so delicious. After grandpa serves us slices of turkey, the other dishes are passed around the table.

Jay is sitting on one side of me, and Ruthie on the other. As I take my third helping of dressing Ruthie kicks my leg at about the same time Ma glares at me from the end of the table. The men and Jay are still eating, why can't I? I ask myself. Most of the talk is about how delicious the food is.

After desert, tea, and coffee we men folk again sit in the large parlor and talk about farming and blacksmithing. The small children play on the floor in front of the stove with their new toys.

Aunt Minnie comes into the parlor to play the pump organ. Jay and I take turns pumping the bellows and we sing carols as Aunt Minnie plays.

Grandma has fixed Christmas stockings for us children. They contain fancy Christmas candy, fruit, nuts, and a small toy. Mine is a yo-yo. Now Jay and I can learn tricks together.

Aunt Mertie brought each child a brightly wrapped package of her famous maple sugar candy. My, that stuff is good!

The festive day ends all too quickly and we begin to gather our things to go home. Pa and I go to harness the team and bring the cutter to the house. As I step into the hall, I hear Grandma Scott saying to Ma, "Ellen, Danny's pant legs, and jacket sleeves are too short. You must get him another suit soon!"